I0603674

In the Dust

Written by
Takani Dillon

Prologue

CHAPTER ONE

It was a Saturday night, and the middling cohort had scurried out of their rat holes to congregate in their friendly neighbourhood pub, as had all their kind across the land from Byron to Broome. They sat in groups and drowned the memories of their long, hard week. They lived for the weekend, suffering five days for the merriment of two. They wore their beer guts proudly and married feeble women with whom they could bestow upon the world a litter of abhorrent little runts, thus continuing the cycle. It's a crying shame not more of them contracted gout.

I walked the streets of my hometown, admonishing every inch, and upon arriving at this grand establishment, stood outside and looked in at the animals. It wasn't my regular scene, but just the same, I'd graced the joint with my sage presence once or twice in the past. I was still a few months away from eighteen and thus lucky for any grog I could get my hands on. One of my old strategies of acquirement had been making my way through the side entrance and swiping unattended schooners as their owners were off playing pool or pissing or doing whatever else those people do. The beer was, of course, terrible – those hapless pricks not knowing hops from dirt, or barley from shit – but beggars can't be choosers, so I'd sneak them out to the adjoining alley, scull the cunts, then throw the empty glasses behind a bush.

On one occasion a few months prior, I was even so bold as to walk right in through the front entrance and up to the bar, cash in hand and a cheery little smile on my dial. I thought it might just work; I had some stubble on my chin and was fairly certain that the publican, a gluttonous old cunt whom the angels named Lenore, didn't know me from Adam. Unfortunately, despite my best efforts in stealth, it turned out that some old barfly had become wise to my side entrance game and informed her of my appearance. I might have left of my own accord if only Lenore had asked nicely, but for some reason she decided to bother the local law enforcement with the matter, and so I ended up in the back of a police cruiser, being driven home to my loving parents. The pig in question, a youngish man I had never seen before, had the audacity to swing by the Bottle-o on his way to picking me up, grabbing a little something for after his shift. My hand to Gan, I saw the shit do it.

My mother looked positively terrified in her little pink nightie as the car rolled up the driveway, but Dad just looked tired. I made my way inside while the piglet gave them the rundown on the front steps. I had expected to be in some trouble, but they didn't seem all that bothered by the situation; I guess they'd given up on me by then. It wasn't the first time I'd been escorted home in a piggy-mobile, you see.

My parents were both ex-financiers who, after making some intelligent investments and subsequently undergoing a faux non-materialist, faux anti-capitalist, and anti-suburbia awakening, had decided to make the ungodly reverse sea-change from Sydney's North Shore to Esk, South East Queensland. I thought disillusioned rich folk were supposed to move to Byron, wear tie-dye and shit, but nooooo ... Here I was in nowheresville instead, with no beaches or loose German tourist chicks for miles. They bought a stunning old Queenslander and renovated out most all of its interior charm, and since I was only young at the time of the move, that house and that town were the only homes I'd ever known.

I never had friends in school, the other kids being as uninteresting as they were, nor did I have luck with the ladies, but nevertheless, I was immensely gifted in the social fields of charm and charisma and used these to build a network of strategic acquaintanceships. This was just the way I liked it; as a substitute for friends, I had literature and music. As a substitute for girls, I had – having grown up in the age of such graphic internet content – access to all the free pornography I could ever want, and plenty that I *didn't* want but was powerless to look away from.

I got into trouble plenty, but I wasn't usually the instigator; I just didn't take shit. So, when some pretentious farmer's kid (as they were the height of the social order in that place and time) would insult my choice of clothing or rip from my hands whatever Penguin Classic I was occupying myself with, the fists would fly and the blood would flow. Being only a small fry of five-foot-nine and skinny to boot, I picked my fights carefully at first, but as my knuckles grew harder and my reputation as a hell-raising little scrapper began to proceed me, I stopped being afraid and thenceforth commenced my inarticulate, lifelong crusade against the brutes.

On one occasion, I got into it with a big, stupid woodmill worker's son by the name of James MacMillan. He threw careless haymaker after careless haymaker as I ducked and weaved and jabbed in between, and then we were broken up by two teachers. It didn't amount to much for either one of us, myself walking away untouched and James with only a few bruises, but we had to sit with the principal in his uninspired little office and talk it out until we were nice and peachy anyway. And then, a few months later, as only Gan could have predicted, my pretty little iPhone went dingy-ding with a text from James. It was a friendly invite to his eighteenth birthday party, and a real bonanza it promised to be, him being the popular type. My initial reaction had been to scoff and dismiss, but then an idea occurred to me.

'Jimmy boy! How ya been, mate?' I greeted cheerfully upon entering his peasantry domicile, approximating as best I could an authentic Occa accent and persona.

James didn't reply. He was standing in the middle of his small back-yard, completely spaced out. From the back portion of his house, one could clearly make out the heightening bushland that stretched past and above our town, Mount Glen Rock being the most dominant feature on display.

'James?' I enquired further, snapping my fingers in front of his fuck-ugly face. He finally turned to me.

'What the fuck are you doin' 'ere?' he replied.

I was confused at first, but when I heard a pathetic little giggle and turned to see a group of his friends watching our happy interaction, I knew what was going on: it had all been a setup, and shit was more than likely about to hit the air-conditioning unit.

So much for being inconspicuous, I thought to myself as I looked around for a clear exit. The original plan had been to mingle with the fools for a short while and then casually slip away with as much grog as I could carry without garnering attention. But just as I was about to go to plan B – grab what I could and make a run for it – James surprised me.

'I s'pose ya can stay if ya don't start shit.'

'Oh, I won't. I just wanna hang and get loose,' I replied with a smirk. He shrugged and went back to his thoughtful stupor. Thoughtfulness didn't suit his face, not one bit. Somehow, it actually made him look dumber.

I used my great and undeniable charm and charisma to mingle seamlessly and actually began to have fun. The small minds that surrounded me were perfect fodder for the sludge I needed to get out of my pretty little head to make room for the more refined, intellectual thoughts.

James had left school halfway through the year to work down at the mill with his father and some other of the area's most impotent degenerates, and a number of the attendees were his co-workers. I made jokes to these people about their friends getting their dicks caught in milling machinery and thereafter undergoing gender reassignment surgery, and other such simple-natured humours, for which they would reward me with cigarettes and beer. I noticed that if I talked fast and hard enough and without my immense charm wavering, I wouldn't have to deal with the repulsive sound and contents of *their* speech, so I went from group to group doing just this and bumming smokes for my troubles. Then, after an hour or so of being the young Carl Barron-ish funny cunt, I saw my golden duck.

I was alone in the kitchen and found in the fridge an untouched sixer of (only slightly shit) beer. I swiped the suckers and exited unseen through the front door.

As I sat on the decaying platform of the town's abandoned train station, drinking my beer and surveying the stars, I couldn't help picturing that thoughtful look on James' face. He had talked to some folks, graciously accepted some happy birthdays and how-do-ya-dos, but he would always wander back to his default position: standing in the middle of his backyard and looking up at Glen Rock.

I was woken at 8 am the next morning by my mother's fist banging on my bedroom door. So invasive was this percussion, she might as well have shoved it up my arse to wake me instead.

'*Go away!*' I groaned.

'*Get up, Edward. We need to talk to you,*' she answered, her elegant, upper-class drawl somehow more anxious than usual.

I climbed out of bed spryly, hangovers not being such a thing in those days, and made my way down the hall, wondering what I'd done this time.

It was late November, and the temperature was formidable despite the early hour. The air quality was also shithouse on account of the nearby bushfires (that particular fire season being one of the worst on record) and so the house was completely closed up, the ceiling fans and air-con doing their work. I hate conditioned air, slight against our sage creators, it is.

I was mildly interested to find in the living room not only my parents, but also two police officers: one of them the cunny old Senior Sergeant MacMillan (James' grandfather) and the other the young Constable who had driven me home after my ejection from the pub all those months ago.

I sat down next to my father as the pigs on the opposite couch offered hellos. *Here we go,* I thought; *what ludicrous curveball is about to be thrown into my day?*

'*Eddy. Can I call you Eddy?*' the old pig asked.

The soft approach; interesting.

'No,' I jested. '*Call me Mr. Sky or get the hell out of my house.*'

No one laughed at my zinger, leaving me feeling cold and stupid. I looked over at my mother, who had risen from her chaise and was pacing the floor.

'*This one's serious, mate,*' said my father, clapping a hand on my shoulder. His face was grave, and it may have been the first time I had seen in him that much care for something that wasn't money or racehorses.

'*Eddy, when was the last time you saw Lauren Grace?*' the sergeant asked.

Wow-wee. This was a curveball, all right. I noticed the pigs studying my face.

'*Probably when school ended. I heard she's got a boyfriend over in Toowoomba, maybe she's staying up there.*' Using the term "boyfriend" was gussying up the facts somewhat. In actuality, if the word on the street was to be trusted, Lauren had fallen in with a bunch of rugby players from the university and they'd been passing her around like she was one of their practise balls.

Lauren was very pretty, in addition to being well-spoken and book smart, and I had always admired her from afar in spite of her devotion to the St. Agnes Anglican Church and burgeoning predilection toward boys of the lower class. At the start of our final year of school, she had begun coming in with dark bags under her eyes, and wearing more makeup than usual to hide the fact. A subtle sign, but visible to those who dare to be observant. She then started missing the occasional day (mostly Mondays), and after a while it had become common for her to skip two or three days at a time. The rumour mill, to which I was well tuned, started spinning yarns abundant, the most reliable sources telling stories of endless partying and inebriation, and also prostitution when the drug money ran out. A wild phase indeed for the holy young lady. Her grades had slipped, obviously. Not greatly at first, but enough to annoy her (little perfectionist that she was) and by the end of spring, it was unusual to see her at school or any of the local hotspots at all.

'*Can you give me a date, a rough one, even?*' asked the old pig.

'*Must've been exam week,*' I answered. She sat a few rows in front of me during our maths final and had been fretting and fidgeting something fierce, as if the better part of her future depended on what she wrote on that page, but whatever party drugs she had been binging recently had reduced her brain to mush. *'Late October. We weren't exactly close.'*

At this, the old pig stopped with whatever had been preoccupying him in his notebook (could've been a nude sketch of my mother, for all I cared) and looked up at me with a stupid smirk. *'What do you mean "weren't"?'*

I sighed deeply. What a fucking drag, what fools I have to share the world with. I looked the pig dead in his simple face and spoke sternly. *'If you're inferring that my use of past tense just now was some kind of Freudian slip, some indication that I know something about whatever's happening with Lauren, you're somehow dumber than you look.'*

No sooner had the words left my mouth than I felt a hard slap across the back of my head.

'A young girl's missing, and you're sitting here making jokes?' my mother screamed. I was too angry and embarrassed to reply.

There was an added tension in the room, and my mother began to pace once more, the wooden floorboards creaking under her slight frame. My father, in his bespectacled and balding haplessness, sat with his head in his hands.

The old pig was staring at me loathingly, as if I were some unpleasant oddity he would rather avoid; as if I were a suspect in some sinister plot; as if, in his mind's eye, he was watching me bludgeon sweet little Lauren Grace with a tyre iron, or perhaps having my way with her tight, young pussy post-mortem.

I met his stare with my own frustrated passion. It must have been an uncomfortable sight for the piglet, who hadn't said a word so far. MacMillan eventually broke the silence.

'Well, I think we've served our purpose here.'

'And what purpose was that?' I enquired, maintaining eye contact as the officers stood to leave.

The piglet walked straight out and down to the cruiser, but the sergeant stopped in the door and turned back to face me.

'Look, Eddy. Something bad has happened to Lauren, something very bad. I can't tell you how I know this, but I do. Are you sure there's nothing you can tell me, mate?'

I didn't believe this. She was fine, just off her face somewhere, nothing serious. The tension in the room was just adults being a (bunch of) dolts; worrying unnecessarily. But in the interest of getting him off my back, I decided to divulge what I'd overheard at the party the night before.

'There is something, and you would've gotten it sooner if you weren't so indignant.' I waited for someone to scold me, but it didn't come, so I went on. *'Katie Bougal said she saw Lauren on Thursday, go talk to her.'*

The useless old pig shot me one last menacing look, then he composed himself and left.

Later that morning, I found my lonesome self back down at the train station. It was an ongoing project of mine to counteract all the idiotic graffiti there with my own mottos of hope and goodwill, balancing slogans such as *D Mac wuz here* and *big lez 4 life* with quotes like *Arm the homeless* and *Exterminate all the brutes.*

The Blues (council workers, as it were, derivative of *blue collars*) did a pretty good job of striking down whatever new acts of youthful expression came up on the walls of our fine public infrastructure, so I knew that my words of wisdom and all the others' creations probably wouldn't last through the middle of next year. Shame it is to live in an age of such confined expression. Such an irony of this world that it's up to the heedless brutes to judge art as legitimate or otherwise – such a terrible irony.

I was in a mood that day to leave a less-temporary mark on my corner of space, so I thought about what surface might be inconspicuous enough for the beady little eyes of the irreverent Blues to overlook. The roof seemed as good a place as any.

I went around back and climbed onto the water tank that stood adjacent to the building, thinking of what I should write. An original piece was the answer. Every sage street philosopher I admired was either dead or aged past relevance, and now it was my time, but what did I have to say? I was a spoiled rich kid from the middle of nowhere. What the fuck did I know about life and the world? I jumped from the water tank to the roof, the thought depressing me. I realized that, due to the wavy surface of the corrugated sheets, I would have to write my message nice and small in between the peaks, but that was okay. It wasn't about being seen. I got out my trusty little permanent marker, but my mind was blank; the goings-on of that morning had castrated me. That fucking dumb-shit sergeant coming to *me* of all people when some chick stops answering her parents' phone calls, and that sour look he had given me ... Typical of the simple-minded to see me as some kind of budding criminal. I think most of the town thought as much. I lie, I cheat, and I steal, but that doesn't make me a criminal. It comes down to intention. Criminals commit crime for the same reason law-abiding citizens go to jobs they hate their whole lives; they're afraid of not having enough. I, however, am *not* afraid – I just do what I want, for no other reason than because I can.

Take the beers I swiped from James' place as an example. The reason I stole them was simple – I wanted to get drunk – and the reason I didn't feel bad about stealing them is that I believe no one can really own anything, and so everything is fair game. Kick rocks and read Sartre if you disagree with me, you belligerent cunts. To be truly free is not to have money or power over others, or to live in a neighbourhood where you can take a midnight stroll safely. To be truly free is to understand that the rules don't apply to you.

<u>Rules are for idiots</u>. This was my tag on the roof, nice and small in between the waves, and it's still there today. Go look, if you don't believe me.

I made to jump back down, but stopped at the last moment; something had caught my eye. Apparently, I hadn't been the only one to have the idea of tagging the roof. There was something written on the far side. I went over to inspect and saw the faded tag, *J LUVS L,* written in sharpie. How fucking sweet. Ain't *LUV* grand?

I jumped down, and something clicked in my brain like a firecracker the moment I hit the ground. J and L – James and Lauren. They had dated for about a week last year. How the fuck had I forgotten?

The young affair had started as something of a secret, but tough luck trying to keep a secret in a high school. That shit was all over the rumour mill in no time. I remember feeling sick when I first heard the rumblings. I couldn't help picturing that big lump of a *torth* tenderly climbing atop that slim, pretty figure. No sense of balance could come of such a union. Disgusting, I say. I had felt even worse when my keen ear happened upon the stories of what she was up to in Toowoomba, my imagination conjuring, as it would, images of Lauren in a small dorm room, surrounded by all those obese athletes and handling their pathetic little dicks in a fashion that in *no* way lived up to her last name.

Perhaps I had been jealous; she was no doubt a fine physical specimen, and I probably would have given it to her good and hard if she had walked up to me and asked for it. Not that I would've known what to do with a woman at that point, immaculate virgin that I was. (I wasn't waiting for the gentle touch of love or something – I was just easily turned off by flagrancy and the ways of the brutes and thots, gallivanting around together as they are prone to do. If I needed a release, I had the internet to turn to.)

It had been hard for me to see Lauren as anything other than pleasant, placid, and for all intents and purposes, *perfect,* up until nine months ago. So, what had caused her to go off the deep end like she had, and why she had stooped so low as James MacMillan on the way down, I had no idea. I pictured the young couple sitting on that red train station roof one starry night, conversing over whatever occupies such minds and perhaps swapping swigs on a goon sack. Perhaps he had told her that her sparkling blue eyes were more beautiful to him than all the stars above before going in for the kiss, or perhaps he had just stared at her in his dumb way until there was simply nothing else left to do. Perhaps something else entirely, I don't fucking know.

My head hurt thinking about it, so I walked home and tried to clear myself, but it was no use; there was some grey cloud.

I returned to a frivolous tirade between my loving parents, who seemed to be fighting more and more. I went into my room and had a right old wank, trying my best to not think of Lauren as I did so, and then a much-needed nap.

I woke two hours later still feeling beat up and tired, but made an effort to rise before I could persuade myself to stay in bed. The rest of that day was drab and not worth my time in describing it to you.

I had strange dreams that night. They were like a series of vivid paintings steeped in surrealism but lacking direction, probably marked by some street whore of a creator who didn't know Da Vinci from DiCaprio and had piercings, tattoos, and chlamydia.

I was bouncing around on a planet made of giant fried eggs, with the starry sky above and the sound of a descending major triad but with each note played in reverse emanating from all around. I came to a cliff and began to carefully climb down, taking occasional bites out of the surface for protein and because I could, but slipped halfway and landed hard. I then found myself in a white room, strapped to a leather chair and surrounded by nerds in lab coats. I was wearing a weird pair of electronic binoculars, which had been pointed at a raw egg in an enclosed agar plate. I was a guinea pig in some sort of visual stimuli experiment.

This invasion of my dreams gave me reason to be angry upon waking, and so I was in a mood for trouble.

My father happened to own a brand-new Toyota Camry, maroon in colour. A boring car for a boring fellow, I suppose. I swiped the keys from the rack by the door as he looked at me curiously over his big coffee mug and Financial Review, but by the time he realised what I was doing and had heaved his steadily bloating frame after me, I was already kicking up gravel at the end of the driveway. He'd be pissed later, but I would deal with that moment when it came. *This* moment was all mine.

I drove into Toowoomba, screaming at the raped mountainside as I reached her outskirts (strip-mined, you see) and reverse paralleled along the main drag, using the built-in rear camera to do so and hating myself for it. Real men park with their wits.

I walked the streets of the small city, falling in love with every woman I passed under thirty, all in their carefree summer dresses and playsuits, none paying much mind of me. I wished one would be mine; just one was all I needed to fix me proper; make a respectable young brute of me and sign me up to Blues apprenticeships and such. Live the simple life of the simple mind.

During my entire foray into the civilization of that particular day and location, I kept expecting to see Lauren strutting around somewhere. I entered each corner in suspense of seeing her on the other side. I conjured a romantic image of her walking the street, her natural blonde hair swaying about, her back straight and her legs long, but I knew in my heart of hearts that if I were to *actually* see her, she'd more likely be stumbling around in some far-off state and/or leading a pack of rugby boys like thirsty dogs.

These thoughts stayed with me as I drove home that afternoon. I wondered what she was up to, admonishing my tendency to quietly worship her as I did so. As sickening as her gluttonous exploits had been of late, I could see her coming out clean on the other side. She was too perfect not to. But that thing Sergeant MacMillan had said, '*Something bad has happened*', had finally begun to worry me.

I thought back to James' eighteenth, a time and place in which I had been such a delightful little manipulator (as I was destined to be until the selfish grave) and remembered the thing I'd overheard.

I had been making my way to the kitchen – a freshly deserted locale in which I was about to look in the fridge and find the free beer – and could vaguely hear three of Lauren's friends, Katie Bougal, Sophie Kane, and Jade Bell, discussing Lauren. Jade and Sophie expressed their concern, saying that they hadn't talked to her directly nor observed activity on her socials recently, but then Katie told them she had seen Lauren the day before, scooting around in the passenger seat of James' old, blue Ford Laser. This seemed to reassure the others. But why would she come back to town just to see *him*? It didn't make sense. No one else had seen her except for Katie, seemingly not even her parents. If she and James had rekindled their old, benign flame, I thought I would have known about it, keen ear to the rumour mill as I had, but I didn't think it was likely.

She's fine, I thought to myself. At best, she was on an epic, you're-only-young-once bender to end all others; at worst, coked out in some drug den and selling her stunning, underage body to the most expedient bidders. Either way, she'd come out clean on the other side.

I decided I was done thinking about it and had about five peaceful seconds, and then, in a flash, I saw everything.

I pulled over to catch my breath. *No,* I thought, *no fucking way*. But there was no ushering the thought away. It was half intuition and half objective observation of the facts, and what it amalgamated to was this: I knew where Lauren was, and I knew how she got there.

My parents spouted an angry duet in my general direction as I pushed open the grand front door, but stopped when they saw my face.

I went straight down the hall and into the bathroom, where I spewed in the shower. Fully clothed, I lay in the bath and turned on the tap, but then decided against the idea and got back out. Dripping wet, I looked myself hard in the mirror and saw how I had managed to shut up my folks. I looked terrified, skin pale and pupils dilated to high heaven.

'*Are you all right, Eddy?*' my mother called from down the hall.

'S-sick,' I somehow managed to croak back.

'*Probably on drugs,*' added my loving father.

With effort, I made it to my bedroom, stripped off my wet clothes, and curled into a shivering ball under the covers, where I stayed for an hour or two.

I finally came to the conclusion that it was on me. What other option was there – tell the pigs and hope they would get it right? I sleuthed out of the French doors that adjoined my bedroom to the verandah and vaulted over the banister, then began my dirge march into town.

The air quality seemed worse than ever that day, and the folk I passed seemed more discontented than usual; possibly due to the air, or maybe they sensed what I sensed. I walked through the well-kept parklands past town, and by the time I got to Sandy Creek, a feeling had arisen. I could sense two different yet equally dreadful forces, one pushing me forward and the other drawing me toward.

I crossed the four-wheel-drive track and walked through the bush and up the slope, my stomach weakening with each step, hoping I wouldn't be sick again.

The day was fading as I neared the peak of Glen Rock, the location that James had been so transfixed by during the night of his party. The two forces reached an intersection, my young self in the middle, wanting both to run away and to freeze in place, yet powerless to do anything but continue forward.

Just as I had finally convinced myself that I was wrong, and that the dreadful forces I was at the mercy of were imaginary, I smelled her.

I turned my head down when I caught the first glimpse through the trees, thinking it would make it less real, thinking that maybe I didn't *have* to look, but I knew I did.

I reached the ridge's edge, my heart beating hard and fast, and brought my head up to face her. Well … There she was, no two ways about it, naked as the day she was born and tied upright to a tree, staring out vacantly over our pretty little town. Her head was tilted to the left slightly, a small lock of blonde hair hanging down over the bridge of her nose, acting as a divider between her once perfect, now glassy, blue eyes. Her lips were green and yellow and forever pursed in a small 'O' shape. Her perky tits were cold and bruised. Her taught abdomen had been torn to pieces and her guts were hanging out every which way, ants and maggots having their feast on what was left. The blood from her midsection had streaked down her legs and left a pool on the ground. Here's the worst part, ladies and gentlemen, and I go to great pains in describing this: It looked as if someone had taken a blade to her pubic bone, a crude attempt to shave off the small tuft of thin, curly hair, and then carved something there with the blade's tip. The writing was small, and it would be impossible to make it out without first cleaning up the blood all around it, but just the same, I knew what it said: *J LUVS L.*

I finally tore my eyes away and stumbled into the bush. I spewed again and lay on the ground for a few minutes, then got up and fucking exploded, screaming hysterically and punching an unfortunate tree over and over again, then I broke down in tears.

There was a stark, white flash, and next thing I knew I was back down at Sandy Creek, washing my face, no memory of descending from the scene.

Then another flash, and I was walking through town, savouring my disassociated hatred.

Then one more flash, and I was in the position I first began to describe before this mighty tangent – standing outside the pub, looking in at the animals, preparing myself to kill James MacMillan.

CHAPTER TWO

I walked in just as *The Boys Light Up* started on the jukebox.

'*Not you again,*' Lenore protested over the loud chatter and music. I barely heard her.

James was sitting alone in the back. I approached him and flipped the table. He stood, wide eyed. I'm sure he knew that I knew. I punched him in the jaw, harder than I have hit *anyone* before or since. The crack was unmistakable and sickening; the cunt would be drinking his beer through a straw from now on. He fell unconscious to the sticky floor. Then came the horde; a group of about a dozen, restraining me and hustling me out-side. Things began to blur, and I thought I was going to whiteout again, but luckily, I was punched hard in the gut and woke to the world some. Lenore-the-tumescent was screaming some useless drivel as I was pushed out of the building, and the last thing I saw of the inside was James, rising to his groggy feet, pushing away one of the kind souls who had gathered around to help him, and running out the back. I was pinned against the exterior wall by some particularly large brute, who was luckily shielding me from the guy who had punched me inside and was now trying to capi-talize on the negative energy to start further shit.

The sirens came quickly, and when the paddy wagon pulled up, I was given a moment of respite as my captor released me, making way for the professionals to take over. I turned and faced the circle of people and then saw Sergeant MacMillan pushing through the crowd. He grabbed me by the throat and handled and cuffed me roughly.

'*Is he okay?*' MacMillan asked the crowd.

'*He ran out back,*' someone replied.

'*FUCKING CHASE HIM!*' I roared.

It was no use. *I* was the villain in that moment, and there was nothing I could do to convince anyone otherwise. The last thing I remember before being pushed in through the tiny door of the paddy wagon was hearing the fadeout of *The Boys Light Up*. All that had transpired had done so during the course of that one song.

The ride back to the precinct was a pleasant moment of solace, but for the intentionally hard right turn onto Highland Street that sent me sprawling to the floor in a cumbersome heap. The hit I sustained during the skirmish was starting to prick at my attention. Actually, it would be more honest to say that it was making me nauseous again. There was one glorious moment when, upon having the tiny door opened for my delicate disembarkment, I thought I was going to spew right down on that wretched old, labia-faced, wrinkled cunt of an old fuck, but he pulled me down fast and started ushering me toward the station, and so I was an unfortunate young man to be held tight and have no place to project but down my shirt and onto my shoes. You might have thought my stomach would have by then been empty, having thrown up twice already, but you would be wrong. In fact, I think that last one was the biggest of the three.

I was grunting like an animal as I entered the mighty enemy's castle, the clerical lady behind the glass screen staring at me with disgust and fear. Could've been Lenore's twin. Maybe she was.

I was processed quickly and escorted to the interview room, where I was left alone for about thirty minutes.

MacMillan eventually returned and took the seat across from me. At first, he just looked at me, the same unpleasant stare he had been so disrespectful to extend my way in my very own domicile the day before. I did my best to show him that I wasn't intimidated, and I think I succeeded. The shock and sickening fear that had so enveloped my being had subsided, leaving in its wake an encompassing coldness. My bruises didn't hurt, and I wasn't self-conscious about the moist lunch remnants and bile on my T-shirt and Doc Martens (say they're for dykes and I'll strike you down); everything was just cold.

'You must've really scared him, mate. Can't find him anywhere. Not at home, not answering his phone. He never hurt anyone,' said the sergeant, still staring at me in that vile fashion. The cadence of his speech was slow and deliberate, clearly a necessary technique to embellish his acute unintelligence.

'I wouldn't be so sure of that,' I started.

'What do you mean?'

I was about to tell him, spill everything I knew out of my cute little lips, but I stopped myself just in time.

'Word around town is he's down at the pub most every night, drinking cheap beer like it's going out of fashion. Given this fact, it would seem to me that he's hurting himself. Maybe one day he'll contract gout, or perhaps severe alcohol poisoning; wither in the dirt with all the other single-celled organisms.'

The sergeant's eyes flared for a moment, but he kept his cool.

'Aren't I supposed to have a parent present for questioning?' I enquired.

'Well, this isn't really an official questioning, just a little chat. Questionings are only needed when there's doubt about what happened, but we have two-dozen witnesses saying you walked in there and attacked without provocation. Seems pretty cut and dry to me, mate. I just wanna ask you one thing. What the hell's your problem with James?' He seemed more frustrated than angry, tired and at the end of his rope. *'And, mate ...'* he continued, rubbing both hands down his fuck-ugly face, *'you better be really careful with your answer, because when you fuck with my family, you fuck with me.'*

I didn't reply.

He did some further staring and then spoke again.

'What happened to your hands?'

I looked down and noticed for the first time how smashed up my knuckles were. That poor tree. *'I thought this wasn't a questioning,'* I spat back.

'Well, it looks like you were in another fight today, so maybe it is.'

'In that case, I will require a lawyer and at least one guardian present,' I replied.

His eyes flared again. He opened his garlic-smelling mouth to speak, but was interrupted by a knock at the door. He shot me one last dagger before rising to his feet and opening it. It was the clerical lady from out front who for some reason seemed to have a distaste for me. The sergeant and his esteemed colleague walked down the hall together, leaving me alone again. I wondered if his whole spiel about *'official questioning'* was legitimate, and if I really *did* require one or both of my parents to be there. I didn't really care either way. Police are, after all, just another group of organized thugs; law and order a construct no more nor less valid than anarchy or white power, just a code by which some people live. I have a code of my own, and one of the foremost guidelines of my code is this – *don't trust pigs, for they are the enemy.* Here are the facts, ladies and gentlemen: All little piggies have bullets, most little piggies are dumb, all little piggies have power, and most of us have none. That's why I didn't tell him about Lauren. He was too stupid; he'd just screw the pooch, probably try to pin it on me or something, and what a drag that would be.

Though my revenge plot against James had been an impulsive failure, I was sure that the law of Gan and The Great Unending would eventually punish him in a way that the law of man could only dream of wetly, reincarnate his sorry arse as an ibis, or something.

After a few minutes of being happily lonesome, my very own parents opened the door and poked in their restless faces. They stood in the doorway, seemingly reluctant to enter, as if to do so would be to acknowledge the situation wholly.

'*Eddy,*' said my loving father, my mother cowering behind him. '*I don't know what happened today, and right now I don't want to know.*' He was trying to be strong, but the look didn't suit him. '*We'll talk about it tomorrow, but your mother and I have decided to not bail you out until then. You'll be spending the night here.*'

My mother began to cry at this. What pathetic fools they were. I guess that's what happens when you value the movements of the stock market above art and the holy word of Sartre.

In reply, I said nothing.

'You're lucky you're still underage, this won't go on your permanent record,' he went on. *'I'll tell you now, though: You have some serious thinking to do, because if you keep pulling these types of stunts, your mother and I have decided that when you turn eighteen, you will no longer be welcome to live in our home.'*

Mother let out a dramatic wail. Father went to lead her away, but she pulled free and managed one last look at me, her eyes pleading to see at least a hint of the little boy I had been, but I just stared at her coldly. They left.

MacMillan came back shortly thereafter, a big ol' smile on his big ol' dial. So I had to spend one night in the clink, no biggie.

He led me to the large, communal holding cell and ever so kindly opened the door for me (what a gentleman).

At least I had some company; inside was a scruffy-looking indigenous guy sleeping in the corner. He probably had some interesting stuff to say. Maybe we could even discuss the pitfalls of the European model of justice – a spear to the leg has always seemed more reasonable to me than imprisonment.

'Sleep tight,' the sergeant's voice echoed back as he reached the end of the hall.

This was my first time in lockup, and I lasted all of twenty minutes. I knew this because there was a small window on the door and a clock on the opposite wall outside. It wasn't the injustice of being punished for a good deed that got to me, nor was it my natural animal aversion to being confined; it was a combination of a number of more innocuous things. Firstly, the beds in there were far too hard. Military-grade thickness were the mattresses, unsuitable for anyone who actually values their individualism. Secondly, the guy in the corner was letting out loud farts on a regular basis. Thirdly, I could just imagine the look on my parents' faces – my father drinking port in his armchair, my mother swaying about hauntingly to *Nina Simone* as she often did – if I walked my skinny little legs through the door that night, a free man despite their best efforts.

I realized I only had one play. It was sure to work, but it went against my code. Ironic that, to secure my freedom, my escape from the heedless brutes that govern, I would have to break this doctrine, but in breaking one of its guidelines, I would ultimately be fulfilling its greater purpose – the very reason I follow it in the first place: to be free. Gan and Sartre work in mysterious ways. Besides, if it wasn't me, it would probably just be some hiker a few months from now, and then, in a practical sense, my suffering would have been for nothing.

I pressed my face against the window and looked down the hall. I would do it now, ultimately because things should be done with haste, but also, I couldn't take another minute of that inhumane bed and those carefree, humid farts.

'*Hey, MacMillan. Get down here.*'

No reply. I continued yelling out for several minutes, and just as I thought everyone had gone home, the piglet who had been palling around with the sergeant showed up.

'*What is it?*' he asked, his tired voice only just penetrating the window.

'*Is he still here?*'

'*No, he went to look for James. Left me with all your paperwork,*' he replied with a smile, obviously trying to relate to me.

I faked my best happy face in return, letting him think he had succeeded.

'*Well, you might as well bin it, I've got something better.*'

He laughed. '*There's only one thing you could have that would get you out of here, dude.*'

I looked at him seriously.

'*Nice try,*' he said with a grin.

I kept up my stare. He then went serious, considering the possibility.

'*Okay, I'll call him if you want, but he'll be pissed if you're faking.*'

Once again, I said nothing. He walked back down the hall and pulled out his phone. I wondered if MacMillan would believe me. In my naivety,

I had thought the matter would receive a grave reception from all, but the young one had been distrustful.

As it turned out, though, MacMillan *did* take it seriously, because he was back in the building and thudding down the hall in no less than three minutes.

'What do you know, you little shit?' he snarled through his big, yellow teeth.

'I know what, where, and who. I could speculate as to why, but I might as well leave that up to you,' I replied calmly, though not as calmly as I would have liked. *'I can show you, but obviously I want my charges –'*

'Of course,' he interrupted. *'Is she okay?'*

In reply, I said nothing.

CHAPTER THREE

I, MacMillan, and the piglet (I learned that his name was Grant) walked through the bush with only their police-issued torches and my wit to illuminate our merry way. It looked different in the dark, taking on a surreal, almost ethereal feeling.

I pointed out the tree I had used as a punching bag, and soon thereafter – I was unlucky enough to see the change in Grant's face as it happened, all wrinkled up in fear and disgust – the smell hit us. I shifted my gaze to MacMillan and saw that his face had only hardened at the stench, and lo and behold, for once he didn't look dumb.

I didn't want to look at her again, I really didn't. I pointed in the direction and hoped they would go ahead without me, but MacMillan grabbed my arm and pulled me along.

Well ... there she was again, the eminent martyr on her paperbark cross.

MacMillan radioed the precinct, and then the three of us stood in silence, waiting for the rest of the cavalry to arrive. I was afraid of two things in that moment. Firstly, I was afraid of looking away, and secondly, I was afraid that MacMillan would turn off his large torch or point it elsewhere, leaving Lauren in the dark. I wondered if MacMillan shared my fear, because he didn't look away either, nor did he move or turn off the torch. I could just make out his thoughtful face in the backlight, probably meditating on the dreadful duty of breaking the news to her parents, or maybe comprehending, seeing everything at once for the first time, as I had done that afternoon.

Grant, on the other hand, seemed unable to look. He was crouched over, his torch off, staring out over the few lights of the town.

As the night rolled on, our happy little party was gradually joined by a coroner and some investigative types, a few more uniforms, and a morose-looking goth chick who worked her photography magic on James' *mise en scene* – his still life – and everything became harder. I was made to stay and rehash the story to the detectives before having my fingerprints taken in a forensic truck parked out on Falls Road. But by dawn, it had been established that none of my dainty fingers had touched her body, and so I should have been let go; made to leave I did, but the two detectives stopped me, claiming that the tree I'd punched, which held microscopic remnants of my skin and blood, was evidence enough to plausibly place me at the scene of the crime at the time it was committed and wanted to have me held in custody. To my surprise, MacMillan stepped in on my account, testifying in front of the detectives and whatever false prophets he held dear that my tattered hands had been just fine and dandy the day before. Apparently, he had made a note of it when he was at my house. Perhaps the piggish old brute was a trifle more observant than I had initially thought.

I walked through town in the crisp morning air, envying the people sleeping in ignorance as I passed their dull houses, and then along Esk-Hampton Road to home.

I slipped in through my French doors and could have remained in my room undetected until a more respectable hour, but I had an immense desire to take a shower and wash away the sweat and vomit.

Upon exiting the bathroom, I was confronted by my parents in their ridiculous satin pyjamas.

'*What the hell are you doing here?*' my father yelped in his crusty-eyed indignance.

'*I live here … for now, at least. Read tomorrow's paper for the rest of the story,*' I answered before walking back to my room. They were too stunned to press the point further.

I had those same fucking Dali-like dreams again, but this time one of the scientists in the lab coats was Lauren, and she was talking to me hurriedly. I knew what she was trying to tell me was important, and so listened eagerly, but whatever she said was gone the moment I woke up. I reached for my over-glorified pocket watch (that is to say, my dandy little iPhone) and saw that it was 6 pm. I had slept thirteen straight hours.

The complacent tones of *Eva Cassidy* met my tired ears as I walked down the hall, and upon entering the semi-open living space, I became privy to a series of pleasant smells emanating from the kitchen.

'*Good morning, Edward,*' said my well-meaning yet uninteresting mother with a smirk, as if her little taunt at my tardiness to the world was one worthy of an audience. She was moving around the kitchen in her slim, delicate way, apparently preparing a feast. There were pots and pans helter-skelter and a chopping board apiece for the respective meat and veggies. There was also a half-finished bottle of red on the bench.

My parents kept a good-sized cabinet of well-aged imports, as well as a small number of *sauvs* from South Australia (barren shithole), but they were trophies more than anything. Dad was mainly a port drinker (may Gan strike gout upon his pathetic soul), and it was rare that Mum would drink at all.

'*I decided to make us dinner. I started making one thing and then thought hell, why not emmpty the frinege …*' she trailed off. '*Maybe we could even use the china. Whaty you think?*' Her voice was a haphazard meander, cadence and her usual snootiness to the wind.

'*Food is food, I'd eat off anything clean,*' I said, taking a seat on one of the bar stools along the bench.

This might be amusing. I couldn't remember seeing my mother drunk before, loosened from her usual puppet strings. Maybe she and I were about to have our first real adult conversation, relate to one another in some way. It often occurred to me how little I knew about my parents, such stiffened drones as they were.

Mother laughed. '*Aww, sweetie. You always have been grateful.*'

Really, that's how I come across? Grateful? Fuck, I was going for something else entirely.

'*Would you like a glass of wine? It's …*' she picked it up and examined the label. '*Merlot, fifteen years. Christ, I was still young then.*'

Mother had never offered me alcohol. I almost refused; it seemed like a bonding thing, and the thought of bonding with this woman made me feel apathetic. But free booze was a precious commodity in my world. It was the first real wine I'd ever tasted, and the last real wine I would taste for a long while. Holy Gan, Sartre, and The Great Unending, was it exquisite.

'*Better than that "Goon" you're used to?*' she jested after my first sip.

'*Goon has its purpose, but overall, yes. This is better.*'

'*I'm glad to see you have some taste. Your father never liked wine, he always thought it too bitter.*'

Ironic, considering what a bitter old prick he was himself.

'*Where is Dad?*'

'*I don't know,*' she replied with disinterest. '*He drove off this afternoon, not a word of goodbye.*'

What a sordid state did surround me. It was tough being so much smarter and more rational than the '*adults*' in my life. Quite a tedious drag, indeed.

'*We called Sergeant MacMillan,*' she continued. '*I have no words … I'm sorry.*'

In response, I said nothing. I had been trying my best to oppress the memories of the day before, and Mother's reminder was more invasive than her apology sincere.

'*Has he found James yet?*' I enquired.

'*No, not last I heard. A lot of your classmates have come forward for questioning, though.*'

That just reminded me of those two smug detectives, wearing their suits in the bush and spitting all sorts of vague questions and ill-inspired accusations. Mother seemed to sense my frustration and dropped it.

The rest of that night was actually somewhat pleasant. We drank wine and ate off the china, and it was all very nice. There *was* the matter of tuning out her indulgent ramblings – playing the victim over the perils of upper-class life with phrases such as, '*money isn't everything*' (easy to say when you have it), and '*the more you have, the more things cost*' (fucking tsk) – and also her yearning to move back to Sydney. But the food and grog were good, and we *did* have some pleasant conversation. It seemed as if we both sensed that the next few weeks would be an absolute circus and that we should have one sane moment together before it got underway, and the absence of the patriarchal port-drinker made it all the more tolerable.

Father didn't come home that night; it wasn't until the following afternoon that he bestowed our happy little domicile with his cheery presence. I saw the Camry from my bedroom as it trundled up the driveway and elected to sneak away so as to avoid the shitstorm of vitriol that would surely come.

Over the next few days, the gossip mill began to teem with ludicrous interpretations of the truth, most of which featuring my lonesome self as some sort of hero figure.

James – now the prime suspect due to some disturbing testimonies of my classmates, which I will not detail – was still missing, and people now seemed to think that I was some pillar of civilian justice; that I had undergone some sort of rogue investigation that had led me to the horrible truth. A natural progression of this narrative was that, if the good little piggy MacMillan had been the one to discover what his grandson had done, it would have either been swept under the rug or pinned on someone else – probably me, given my close proximity to the affair and my previous reputation. It seemed that I had garnered, in my little corner of the world, something of a good name. Funny how stupid people are, but whatever; a few more citizens being distrustful of law enforcement could only be a good thing.

I'd be lying if I said it didn't feel good, though; my new reputation. The bad boy with a moral compass, a timeless obsession of my fellow citizens of this great, stolen commonwealth. Ned Kelly, Chopper Read – same shit, different names.

The story made it to the local newspaper, of course, and was covered by a savage young journalist fresh out of uni and trying to make a name for herself. She really sunk her teeth into Sergeant MacMillan, calling his involvement in the case a *'brash conflict of interest'* and insinuating not only that he may have known something before I found the body, but also that he may now know where James was hiding. I knew this was all sensationalist shit, but I liked it nonetheless.

James' father was fired from the mill, an innocent bystander possibly, but fuck the innocent. Let it be his individual punishment for all the raped trees.

Lauren's parents hadn't been seen all week, but some local do-gooder started going around town collecting donations to help with the funeral expenses and such, and my father donated a *very* generous amount. The whole matter had really seemed to stir him from his even-keel default. Maybe there actually was a heart (be it likely clogged) in that rib cage, or maybe she had just given him wood, been his go-to fantasy when diddling my mother or something. Fucked if I know.

I knew of an opinion floating around that I should continue my investigative foray and look for James myself. A part of me wanted to, to finish what I had started in the pub, but no. I am not a calculating person, only impulsive.

Anyway, this isn't some revisionist, post-modernistic, unlikely-boy-idealist-turns-hardboiled-detective story. You can fuck right off if that's what you were hoping for. This is a story about life, and this prologue, just one little speck in a filthy universe.

By the end of the week, the bloodlust for the absent James had died down a bit, the funeral having come and gone and the mourning period (for those not close to the family, at least) drawing to a close. But the people didn't want to go back to their dull normalities. They had been given a taste of an intriguing new world, and they wanted more.

Lenore, the publican waste, had sworn that whilst locking up on Thursday night, she had seen the notorious young man in the flesh, strutting down the main street and belting out *Ave Maria*. This one gave people something to talk about.

There were other such false sightings, but ironically, the first citizen to see James again was none other than yours truly.

On Sunday afternoon, as I was making my way to the only respectable dining venue in our happy community (the Thai place at the end of Ipswich Street), I saw the paddy wagon I had taken a ride in a week earlier swerve out of Highland Street and to the left, sirens ablaze and speeding through the middle of town for all to see and hear. He could have just as easily taken a cruiser and driven quietly; this probably would have been the smarter move, in fact, but the sirens and the paddy wagon and the speeding had created an expectation.

I got my takeaway and sat outside the station, but after an hour it was starting to get dark and it seemed my waiting would be for nothing, so I dropped my eating utensils in the recycling and went to walk home. As I reached the corner of Highland and Ipswich, however, I saw the paddy wagon moving towards me, slowly and without the loud pony show this time. It took the right turn easily, a stark contrast to the jolt that had thrown around my sorry arse the week before. Apparently, it's a good ruffling of your feathers for petty assault and a nice, comfortable ride for murder.

I ran toward the vehicle as it pulled up and withdrew my phone. There he was, the man of the moment. Pale, skinny, and with his jaw hanging askew. The sergeant gave me a daring look as he assisted his grandson out of that tiny door.

'Where've you been, Jimmy boy? We all missed you,' I taunted. 'Good job, Sarge. I hope you get a medal for this.'

I patted MacMillan Senior on the back. At my touch, he turned at me angrily, but he knew there was nothing he could do, not on camera. I followed them inside, capturing even the bewildered look on the face of the admin clerk before the happy chaps made their way through the locked door and down the hallway. I then went home.

The rumour mill was once again a festering mess when I woke the next morning. I heard from a semi-reliable source that James had been held up in some old farmhouse. As the story goes, a farmer by the name of Henry Blythe had gone to a sparsely visited corner of his acreage where the old family homestead happened to be located, all dilapidated and overgrown, and saw an old, blue Ford Laser parked outside. He crept up and looked in through a window, and the sight that befell his eyes was a young man, huddled in the corner and eating a live rat. I believed all of this except for the part about the rat.

There was a lot of further misinformation that day, but most of it was put to rest when the news broadcast their comprehensive account that evening. The report started with a recap of what had happened prior to James being found, then they showed my video of him being brought into custody (I had negotiated a few hundred bucks for their exclusive rights to the footage), then an interview with the senile-looking old farmer coot before finally going into the official press conference with the exhausted-looking senior sergeant. He confirmed that James had confessed to the murder and rape of Lauren Grace (the semen found by the forensics team had been kept hush-hush until then) and that bail would not be set. He didn't go into much detail past that.

When the report ended and the anchor had moved on to an update about the bushfires, there was a stark moment in which I realized it was all over – everything wrapped up in a gruesome little bow, with no more left to ponder or cross-examine. The people would claim they would never forget and that they would never let something like this happen again, but of course, eventually they *would* forget, and whether it happened again or not was completely out of their control. Such is the nature of humans and this world. So yes, it was definitely over.

What a drag. I was ready to put that sorry town behind me then and there, but that would have to wait a few months.

Welcome to the Big Smoke

CHAPTER FOUR

My birthday came in early January. I woke up in the late morning to an elegant breakfast prepared by my mother, immediately after which – I hadn't even finished chewing my fucking scrambled eggs – my father handed me a one-hundred-dollar note and an eighteen-year bottle of Chivas (his idea of a joke, I think – a cheapish whippersnapper of a beverage teetering on the brink of maturity) before opening the grand front door and giving me a friendly *'On ya go, mate,'* motion.

I grabbed my suitcase, having known it was going to happen and having packed the night before. I hadn't exactly cleaned up my act since our little conversation in the cop shop; just the usual shit: showing the brutes who's boss (fighting), liberating silly-juice (stealing alcohol), artful expression (vandalism), etc.

I walked out of my home and into the blue. The moment would have been perfect, if not for the strange whimpering sounds my mother was making upon watching her little boy become a type of man she was too frivolous to understand or be proud of. Still, though, I had never felt so free.

You'd better watch out, world. Eddy Sky is coming to kick in your teeth and press his worn Doc Martens on your pathetic neck until you give him exactly what he wants. And what *did* I want? A redundant question; I wanted *everything*.

I walked to the end of Ipswich Street and out of town, again without looking back or saying goodbye, like a rehabilitated animal being released back into the wild.

I made to walk around the northern tip of Wivenhoe Dam, but sooner hitched a ride with a retired (possibly senile) professor. I was excited at first to have finally met an intellectual, some spark of the outside world, but all he wished to discuss in detail was Schopenhauer's biological theory on pederasty – ironic, seeing as when we arrived in Samford (his desti-nation and town of residence) he placed a spotty old hand on my leg and asked if I'd like to *'Chill in my pool, my dude.'* I suppressed my desire to knock the dwindling light out of the old cunt and politely declined.

From there, I walked the narrow shoulder of Samford Road, and after two hours of huffing and puffing (regular smoking being my general downfall) ended up in the suburban wastelands of Ferny Grove, the west-ern edge of the city limits.

I attracted the eager eyes of many of my fellow passengers as I rode the train further into the hellish and heedless conurbation, but it wasn't the distrustful, non-understanding look I had often been the subject of back home; it was more of a weary, *'The world's coming for you, kid,'* look. Distrustful, but without the fear and reproach.

I suppose I *was* something of a sight: a skinny, sweaty, sunburnt young man in tight black jeans, a T-shirt depicting Brigitte Bardot but with dol-lar-signs for eyes, and a demeanour that lay somewhere between *'Don't fuck with me'* and *'What the fuck are you looking at?'*

The suburbs became more respectable as I rolled along; still wretched slums, but now with small pockets of wealth, no doubt housing the city's lawyers and financiers and psychologists. At least I hadn't grown up there – whitewashed I may have been, my friends.

I was glad to depart when the snake reached Central. I wheeled my suitcase out onto platform three, up the stairs (I don't trust lifts nor esca-lators), and out into the city. It all seemed so big back then, so impossibly dense and alive.

I made a point to stare threateningly at every suit I passed. I even had to spit at the feet of some bearded, philosophical-looking cunt in a Gucci when he dared to laugh at me, unfazed. This particular one was interesting.

It wasn't all cynical drudgery, though. I was having a splendid time. I walked around for hours, memorising the geography, taking in the glut-tonous consumerism of Queen Street, conversing with whichever locals would give me the time of day (not many). It was all an experience, but by

7 pm, my feet were blistered. I figured I might as well go the route of most freshly minted adults and have myself a legal beverage, see if it tasted any different. I conferred with my trusty little iPhone and ascertained that Fortitude Valley would be the perfect place for a seething little degenerate such as myself, and once there, approached the first dingy basement bar I came across.

'*Hold up, dude,*' said the MMA-looking bouncer brute, unwisely grabbing the back of my collar and halting my forward motion. '*I gotta card ya.*'

I suppressed my ingrained desire to scream and swing and instead handed him my licence.

'*New in town,*' I said as he snatched it from my hand and placed it in the boxy mechanism I had initially thought was a breathalyser.

'*Step in front here, it needs to take ya portrait.*'

I did as directed, smiling nice and wide.

'*Ya gonna behave tonight?*'

(Fuck you and all your friends.) '*Of course, I'm a well-behaved young man.*'

He dared to laugh at me. '*Heard that before, than I find yuz doin' coke in the shitta.*'

(I'll do whatever I feel.) '*No, not me.*'

He looked me up and down, said, '*All right. Stay safe,*' then handed back my licence. '*And happy birthday.*'

It took all my power to twist my face into a friendly gesture. '*Thanks.*'

The nerve, the incredible nerve of that burly little bitch to wish me happy birthday. Disgusting.

The joint was dark and dreary – just my scene – with a wide array of patrons that varied from scenester fools to normal-looking and everything in between. I remembered that *Lou Reed* line about the city being a funny place; it's true.

I got a beer and sat at the bar, and being a weeknight, it was quiet enough that I could enjoy the drink in peace. That was, at least until a tall, hippy-looking dude with long, black dreadlocks, ridiculous rose-coloured fashion specs, torn-up jeans, and no shoes sat beside me, right beside me. As I said, the bar was empty – he could have taken any other seat.

'*Tonic water and lime,*' he ordered of the barkeep.

I looked him over, both offended and curious.

'*Drink of true men. Say any different and you'll simply be wrong,*' he informed me without looking my way. '*A fire engine's good as well, if you're feeling frisky.*'

'*Is that so?*' I enquired.

'*Yes,*' he replied, now meeting my gaze.

The contrast of the pink glasses and the serious, almost confrontational demeanour threw me. It reminded me of that old anecdote about a kung-fu master who always wore a pink shirt in hopes that someone would instigate a fight with him.

'*What's with the glasses?*' I asked.

'*What do you mean?*'

'*Why are you wearing them?*'

'*I don't understand the question,*' he said calmly. '*Are you asking if they're prescription?*'

'*Are they?*'

'*No,*' he replied, breaking eye contact to focus his attention on the drink that had just been placed in front of him. '*You can't ask vague questions and expect specific answers, kid.*'

'*Who are you calling "kid"?*'

'*I'm calling you kid, kid. Do you see any other kids around here?*'

'*I'd suggest you shut your dirty fucking hippy mouth if you know what's good for you,*' I said in a raised tone, attracting some attention. Seemed like this cunt was about to feel the sting of my pent-up rage from the bouncer and that bearded penguin and the old pedo-professor.

'*That was a double negative, and I am not a hippy, and I will not shut my mouth.*'

'*You are, and you'd better.*'

'*I wish I was a hippy. Those guys get chicks like you wouldn't believe.*'

During the escalation of our conversation, the strange young man had done nothing but stare passively at his drink. He would rotate it at eye level, throwing his words at me offhand. It was quite odd, and the thing he said about hippies getting girls? That couldn't possibly be true. Hogwash. Nice try, pal.

He then gulped down his beverage in one easy movement before rising to his feet.

'I'm out, this particular interaction bores me. Good luck with your beer,' he said before chucking the small lime in his mouth (skin included) and walking his queer and barefooted self outside.

Welcome to the city, Eddy. My oh my, what a funny old place.

CHAPTER FIVE

I hit the pavement again the next morning, feeling well rested despite having spent the night in a horribly thin-walled backpackers.

I now had to complete the harrowing task of trudging down to the department of human services (note the strategic non-capitalisation; they neither care about humanness nor are they reliable enough to be accurately described as a 'service') and sitting around with a bunch of unemployables and struggling artists – that is to say, I was lodging a welfare claim.

The stench upon entering the building was immense, a gross cocktail of cheap air conditioning and lower-class sweat. Man-oh-man, did I not belong there. There were about four (fat-fuck) individuals who had seized the waiting area as a location for family affair, their decrepit runts either running and screaming or blankly attached to iPads. One was even bound by a leash and harness.

I approached the dead-eyed receptionist and explained the purpose of my presence, but she was challenged by my queries and ushered me to a computer bank on the far wall. *What a terribly impersonal system,* I thought. I filled out the electronic application quickly and – for some stupid reason – honestly, including the section entitled *Parental Income.* I then went back to the receptionist and politely asked for my motherfucking money, but she was again challenged and informed me that I would be contacted.

Naïve me. I thought I could simply walk in there, use my irresistible charm on some null caseworker for a bit, then leave with my Velcro wallet filled. But there was to be some more hoop-jumping, it would seem. A lesson to be learned in life is that shit ain't free, especially money.

That night I went back to the same basement bar. I could tell you the name, but it wouldn't matter much; they're all the fucking same. I bought a beer and pondered the finer points of existence and finances, and half-way through the offensively expensive schooner, I looked to my left and saw the grand entrance of the man I'd met the night before, same pink glasses on his stoic mug. He sat at the opposite end of the bar this time and I thought maybe I'd scared him. He ordered his same old drink and didn't pay me much mind, which was fine with me. I ignored him and continued my ponderances, the most prevalent of which being how long it might take for the system to gift me the money to which I was entitled. *Not too long* was my personal preference, my *current* cashola situation being far from peachy. Maybe I'd have to resort to petty crime, break-ins and such. *Yea, I could leave a copy of* The Age of Reason *in their houses, help them understand. I'd be a modern-day, Robin Hood-like cunt, only roll ignorant folks who deserve it anyway,* I thought.

This fantasy lasted for a minute or two, then it subsided suddenly and I laughed in spite of myself. Who the fuck was *I* to judge deserving from not so? The seventeen-year-old me wouldn't have cared either way; he would have just as easily taken a dollar from a filthy bum as he would from some penguin. Probably would've swiped one of his *Big Issue* copies to skim through later, as well, but the eighteen-year-old Eddy Sky was moral all of a sudden. It made me sick to think of what I had become.

I finished my beer and looked over at the hippy, who was now sucking on a vape. I was highly offended.

'*What the fuck are you doing with that thing?*'

The dreaded fairy looked over at me disinterestedly, then turned away.

'*What flavour, pink fairy floss?*' I needled.

'*No, mint,*' he replied.

'*I thought these places got all indignant if you started blowing smoke around.*'

'*It's mist,*' he replied.

I laughed at this. '*Why don't you smoke cigarettes like a real man?*'

'*Well, I guess I'm not a real man by your standards, but also, I'm not a fuck-ing idiot, so that probably plays a large part, too.*'

I stared at him silently for a good thirty seconds, but he didn't flinch, just kept swirling round his drink and sucking on that flippant device.

'I don't get you, man,' I finally said.

'That's nice,' he replied before downing the rest of his tonic water and walking out the door.

'What's up with that guy?' I directed at the barkeep. He shrugged in reply.

In the late afternoon of the next day, I found myself walking over the Story Bridge to go to the jazz bar on the other side. A fucking jazz bar, who would have thought – a wild spectacle for a sheltered country boy such as I.

Halfway there, I felt a little *buzz-buzz* as my over-glorified vibrator spasmed in my pocket. I looked down at the text message in disbelief. I can't remember the exact wording and I will not attempt to approximate it, but it was from the department of human services and it read, in so many words, *you are fucked because your parents are rich cunts. Welfare claim denied.* I screamed down into the chocolate-coloured river, then I turned around, suddenly dissuaded from the jazz idea, and headed back to The Valley.

I stopped out front of my familiar basement bar and considered, but no, a new place would be better, somewhere I wouldn't have to deal with *Mr. La-Vie-en-Rose.*

I found my new place, a ground-level affair and slightly cleaner than my old go-to, and took a seat. No sooner had my doughy butt hit the cushion than I smelt his essential oil stench and heard his deepish voice. I turned and saw the lanky hippy in the flesh, strutting confidently through the front door.

'Fuck, man, you're everywhere.'

He ignored me and sat at the bar's halfway point, me being on the far left, and ordered a red fire engine. He spent several minutes examining and rotating the drink before taking his first sip.

'Any vodka in that?' I asked.

'*Man, you ask so many unnecessary questions.*' He looked at me and sighed, then looked forward again. '*The short answer is, no.*'

'*What's the long answer?*'

'*More or less the same.*' He turned to me again and this time didn't look away. '*Let me ask you something. What's your name?*'

'*Eddy.*'

'*And your last name?*'

'*Sky.*'

'*Eddy Sky, Eddy Sky, Eddy Sky,*' he repeated. '*Let me ask you this, Eddy Sky. What was the best single beverage you've had in your life?*'

An odd question, but I gave it due consideration and realised I had an answer.

'*Probably the first drink I swiped from the Bottle-o. I went round the back and made some noise, then when the shopkeep came to investigate, I ran round the front and took the first thing I saw – some cheap-shit beer, but it tasted great.*'

He nodded approvingly. '*Cute, that's a cute little story. Now imagine this, Eddy Sky. Imagine you're there – drinking that beer, enjoying the moment, as one does in the middle of the best drink of their life – and then some petulant little hick-dickhead comes along and asks you if it has any vodka in it.*'

I stood up. But just as I was about to push him hard off his stool and pour that red fire engine all over his filthy dreads and face –

'*You're young, though. Still time to learn better. Let me buy you a drink.*'

I never say no to free grog – it's one of the finer points of my code – so I unclenched my fists and sat back down. Imagine my disappointment when he ordered me plain old orange juice.

'*Now swirl it round a bit, get the pulp in motion.*'

I did as directed. Who the fuck was I talking to?

'*Good work, it's ready to take a sip now.*'

I took a sip.

'*Too big,*' he said soothingly. '*Try again.*'

I took a smaller sip.

'*That's better, now wait ninety seconds.*'

I waited a minute and a half before taking my next sip, all the while under his watchful eye.

'*Good work, Eddy. Now repeat this cycle. You can do seventy-five seconds if you're thirsty. I'm gonna go take a shit, watch my drink.*'

I don't know why in the holy names of Gan and Sartre I did the two things he asked of me, why I didn't just scull my drink and his and then run along, but I did.

When he got back, he seemed impressed by my progress. He sculled the rest of his fire engine.

'*Why was that the best drink you've ever had?*' I asked as he stood to leave.

'*Every drink is the new best. It's called optimism,*' he said, handing me his business card. '*Call me if you're ever looking for work.*' Then he left.

I looked down at the card in my hand. It was eggshell white, and the only words written on it were the name *Sunbeam River,* a phone number, and an email.

I finished my orange juice at a normal pace, wondering what the hell kind of business this aloof hippy-cunt might run. Probably some trendy tech start-up; either that, or a drug ring.

CHAPTER SIX

So there I was, standing on a Paddington backstreet outside of a beat-up old Queenslander – dripping with sweat, having walked from the boarding house in South Bank in which I was now staying – and slightly bewildered at the sight before my eyes.

The fences around the property were tall, and it was only after I'd opened the front gate that I could see up to the high-set front verandah, standing on which was my soon-to-be boss Sunbeam River, buck naked and holding a terrified-looking Eshay kid against the wall by his throat, his free hand clenched in a fist and waving manically in front of the kid's face. It reminded me of when MacMillan had held me against the pub wall, all the brutes watching dumbly.

I began walking up the stairs to assess the situation, but by the time I was halfway there, and before I was in earshot (Sunbeam was whispering at him, in contrast to his loud physical movements) he let go and the kid ran down past me, trying to keep himself from sobbing and just barely succeeding. Sunbeam stood proudly at the top, watching the little runt exit the front gate and run down the street.

'*Tough love,*' he said to me as I reached the top of the stairs. He was amazingly hairy; chest, face, other parts I had only caught glimpses of ...

'*Yeah, right,*' I replied.

'*How've you been, Eddy? I'd give you a hug, but it looks like you swam across the fucking river on the way here.*'

Fine with me; I try to avoid hugging naked men whenever possible.

It was just past 9 am, but already thirty-five, dry, and smoky. He led me through the front door and I was relieved to be met by the strong downward draft of a beautiful ceiling fan at top speed. He seemed to read my mind.

'I fucking loathe air conditioning. Runs up the power bill like a slut on a mechanical bull.'

Well, an entirely different reason to those I harboured against aircon, but a common opinion just the same.

The front room was a kind of reception/waiting area. There were white leather couches and a nice coffee table in the middle, even a big fish tank on the back wall with some tropical-looking dudes gallivanting away their meagre lives. *Back and forth. Back and forth. Back and forth. Beautiful skin, but back and forth.*

Off the front room was a well-kept office with a big, pine desk in the middle. I was motioned to sit on the nearside chair while Sunny walked around to the far side, myself getting an unfortunately intimate eyeful of his jungle-like arsehole as he bent to pick up a pair of red, checked boxers on the way. He put them on and sat.

'So, Eddy Sky. E-ddy Sk-y. You want to work for Sunbeam River?'

I knew the question was rhetorical, but I answered anyway. *'Maybe, but it's still not clear what you do here, and also, I'm naturally distrustful of anyone who refers to themselves in the third-person. If that IS your real name, I mean.'*

'Okay. Firstly, of course it's my real name. But you can call me Sunny.'

'I'll call you whatever I please.'

'No, you won't. You'll call me Sunny. Secondly, I thought you were smart. I thought you would have known by now what WE do.'

I looked around the office. It was clean, the *feng shui* was sensible, and there was a smell of lemon grass.

'I have one idea, but in light of how your house looks, it's too ridiculous to be true.'

He laughed. *'There are many things wrong with that statement. Here at Sunbeam Solutions, we're all about professionalism.'* He rested his hands behind his head, revealing his underarms and even more hair. *'Don't let belligerence get in the way of a great opportunity. You could be here with me, or you could be sweeping loose chips and simplex scabs off the floor of your local McDonald's.'*

'And how would that be any worse than sweeping floors here?'

'*We already have a cleaner, thank you. Her name is Lisa, she is lovely, and she uses a vacuum. We also have an in-house chef, who happens to also be our bookkeeper, and a masseuse that comes in twice a week, but I'll rip your fucking ears off if you ask her for a happy ending.*'

'*And what about superannuation?*' I jested.

He smirked. '*The truth is, Eddy Sky, I have bigger plans for you,*' he said, leaning forward and resting his elbows on the desk. '*I need an operations manager; someone I can trust. You're the perfect candidate. Smart, but not too smart.*'

'*Fuck you.*'

'*No, not fuck me. You'll do day-to-day stuff and take care of any wayward vendors, leaving me free to focus on the big picture.*'

I considered.

'*I'm not much for administrative tasks –*'

'*You'll learn,*' he interrupted.

'*– and from what I saw on the way in, you seem to be doing a good job of the latter on your own.*'

'*No, I'm too nice,*' he replied. '*These kids are crafty cunts. They need constant threat, a real mean figure up their smooth little arses.*'

'*And that's me?*'

'*In between admin tasks, yes.*'

I considered again, but not for too long this time. The world had placed me in a delicate position. I could either a) accept some middling job that was far below me, b) stay in my shitty boarding room and twiddle my thumbs until I starved, or c) count out baggies and beat up children for *Sunbeam Solutions*.

'*Okay, where do I sign?*'

I meant it as a joke, but he answered very seriously.

'*Nowhere. Ever.*'

Sunny and I sat in the kitchen and celebrated with a cup each of warm milk. That's right, folks – thirty-five degrees outside and there we were, drinking warm milk. It curdled in my stomach as he toured me around the sizeable house. The first place we went was the *'mail room'*, a large rectangular space in which half a dozen men and women sorted the bulk deliveries into small, sellable quantities. They smiled cheerily as I met them one by one.

The room contained three large dining tables set in a horizontal row – one for weed, one for coke, and one for others (mainly party stuff and white collar/soccer mum shit).

'We don't peddle anything detrimental to our great society; smack and such. That shit's risky anyway; syndicated,' Sunny told me as we left the room.

I nodded as if I understood.

I wasn't too impressed by the scope of the operation; I just presumed this was how it worked in the big, bad city. I had dealt a bit in school, but it wasn't really my thing; I hadn't needed nor wanted the money, and the suppliers were all sketchy losers.

The next room we went to was small, completely lacking in natural light, and with hundreds of mobile phones stacked helter-skelter. It was populated by three young, nerdy types, two at a repair station and one at a computer.

'This is a little side interest of mine. Acquire "broken" phones, fix and flip.'
'Sounds profitable.'
'Very much so,' he replied with a gross wink.

Again, I nodded as if I understood.

Our final stop was a long sleepout area that had been converted into an office space. There were three people in there, all women, but really only one to whom I was able to pay any attention.

Her name was Sandra. Her eyes were green and vague, the skin around them pleasantly tired. Her hair was dark and unkempt. She was wearing a tie-dye singlet and no bra, exposing her tattoo sleeves, hints of her hairy underarms, and a bold suggestion of droopy tits. She wore a content, far-away smile; her foremost feature. I thought to myself that she could have been Sunny's sister. I found out later that day she actually was.

The rest of the morning was filled by Sunny explaining to me the ins and outs of the business and my new role within it, though I got bored and checked out at various points, and then came lunch.

As it turned out, Sandra was the bookkeeper/chef that Sunny had referred to earlier, and as it is said that the way to a man's heart is through his stomach, I waited eagerly to fall for her even further. What was eventually slopped down on my plate was an orange sludge that induced no feelings of hunger upon sight (what the fuck are lentils?) but I gave it a shot and it tasted decent enough.

I put on my best sweet-village-boy routine as the whole *Sunbeam Solutions* family ate on the back deck, my charming young self having been sat right next to Sandra, and it seemed to be working.

'*So, Sandy dear, what's your secret to eternal beauty?*' I heard my smitten self spouting bodaciously.

'*Xanax,*' she replied with a smirk.

Hubba-Hubba, baby. *I'll* save your life.

Sunny didn't protest my playful flirtations. Actually, he seemed amused by them.

When lunch was over, I helped Sandra with the dishes. This gave me a chance at a more intimate approach. She was three years older than me, studying microbiology at uni (her life's ambition being to own the world's largest collection of hallucinogenic mushrooms), and she wasn't joking about the Xanax. These were the facts I gleaned from our conversation over the sink, her washing and me drying. Perhaps I should come to work tomorrow with a rose in my teeth.

The afternoon flew by with more learning (or pretending to look interested) about business processes, as well as doling out supplies to the vendors who came by after school – though the kid Sunny'd had by the neck that morning never showed – and by 5 pm, it was time to go home. What a fucking day and what a fucking business.

Sunny hadn't been joking about professionalism. The bureaucracy of that place was a rife old beast; lots of paperwork and such, which was always shredded and burned at the end of the week anyway.

As I got off the bus and returned to the boarding house, the strange thought occurred to me that I was just another fucking suited sell-out, but the $1500 Sunny had given me (my first week's pay in advance) was weighing on my pocket heavy enough that I was able to push the thought aside. $1500 felt like so much money back then.

CHAPTER SEVEN

'*I guess this is how the grownups do it,*' is what I told myself as I waited in some trendy vegan burger joint on Brunswick Street.

How dishonest it is, this whole dating scene; sitting around with someone who has different genitals to you and pretending it's not awkward. A gross societal formality, but an apparently necessary precursor to the animal act of the early hours.

This isn't to say that I knew how the kids had done it, immaculate virgin as I was, but when has ignorance ever stopped me from passing judgement and casting aspersions?

It was early February, and I had somewhat settled into my new life. Work was a bitch and my weekly wage had been halved due to '*Hard times ahead, my brother. Just watch the news.*' Sunny had followed this with, '*Stick with me now, and we shall prosper together when the red tide does turn ... cunt face.*' What a fucking poet, an eminent *Wordsworth* with a drug empire to his name.

Fuck it all, was my line of thought. $750 was still a princely sum, and I figured that, in this particular game, employment was always a shaky proposition. Hell, it would probably end with me stomping the big, hairy cunt anyway.

I had moved out of the boarding house and into a shitty little furnished apartment on Alfred Street. I looked at nicer places at first, but as it turns out, agents and landlords are distrustful of young scrappers who can only pay in cash. The place I found was good enough; a softish bed, a small kitchenette, a window overlooking the street, and all mine, if I continued to slap down two green pieces of polymer plastic into the greasy old hands of my greasy old landlord every Friday. Happy days. There was an aspiring oboist next door who seemed to practise at every hour, but apart from that ... happy days.

In my spare time, I would usually just walk the streets and wait for something to happen. Something always did.

I'd sometimes go to this sleazy massage parlour and give a friendly Thai girl with terrible breath seventy bucks, and for that she would get out an oil-based lube and jerk me off until I came all over myself. She would then wipe me clean and avoid eye contact as I thanked her and left. I always felt dirty afterwards, but revisionist history is a strong point of mine, and so I'd always end up back there a few days later.

I never took the plunge into full-blown prostitution, astute moralist and sage puritan that I am, and things with Sandra had been heating up anyway, so (some of my loving parents' financial smarts must have rubbed off on me) why pay for what might soon be free?

The light office flirtation had culminated in my brave little self taking the initiative and asking her if she'd want to go out sometime, because that's what grown-ups do. Now she was late. Fucking typical, just like her brother; professional during work hours and flaky as shit outside of them.

I was about to get up and leave, maybe see if that massage parlour was open, but then she walked through the door and all my frustration regarding her arrogant tardiness dissipated. She was wearing a plain black T-shirt and seemingly a bra underneath. A rarity that was; the girls looked perky for once. She also wore tight blue jeans and black converse, and her long, messy hair was back in a ponytail. For the first time while in my presence, she looked more or less normal. Not for the first time in my presence, she was very beautiful. She sat across from me.

'Hi, Eddy.'

'Sandra, my dear.'

I left an efficient amount of silence to allow her to apologise, but she didn't take me up on the offer.

'I like it when you talk that way – all proper. It's cute.'

Cute, huh? Well, I was going for sophisticatedly sexy, but beggars can't be choosers, I guess.

'You're very kind.'

She released her handbag from its perch on her shoulder and placed it on the table. It was a little brown thing with a huge, golden clip, a positively ridiculous sight to anyone with taste.

'What're you smirking at?' she enquired whilst rustling through the tiny bag.

'Nothing, just a joke I heard earlier.'

'Who even tells jokes these days?'

'Mostly people who aren't that funny.'

She laughed at this and *finally* retrieved her phone (fucking Pandora's box that bag was). She put it on silent and placed it face down on the table, then looked up at me and let out a sigh.

'Big day at work,' she said.

'What do you mean?'

The standard office hours at *Sunbeam Solutions* were the dreaded and celebrated 9 am to 5 pm, Monday through Friday. Today was a Saturday.

'There's a potential situation, I had to do some boring numbers stuff.'

'Why wasn't I called in?'

'It's not really an ops thing. Sunny will fill you in. Let's not talk about work, yeah?'

'Okay then. Would you like a drink?' I asked in the tone that she apparently thought cute. She said she would.

I was still getting used to the concepts of a) being able to drink legally, and b) paying for grog as opposed to swiping it. I got carded regularly, and as I approached the bar, I was hoping to shit that they wouldn't do it then, Sandra being by my side. Thankfully, they didn't.

The night started with us having a beer together. I appreciate a girl who appreciates a beer, but an uncomfortable and unfamiliar feeling had begun to creep up on me those previous few weeks, and I felt it then – drinking with her and bullshitting about this and that – most strongly. The feeling was contentedness, and I had no idea what to do with it.

When our burgers came, I was slightly disturbed by the greenness of the buns, but upon taking a bite of the thing I thought that maybe the pussy vegans might know some shit after all. Best fucking burger of my young life, it was. Green buns withstanding.

We ate and we talked and we drank some more, and it all felt good. I felt that night the way Sandra looked; more or less normal. Not an effective frame of mind in the long run, but a nice thing in which to delude myself briefly.

After dinner, we made our handsome way to a certain rooftop bar (again, I could tell you which one, but it wouldn't matter – they're all the same) for more heavy beverages and light conversation. Not that there was any chance of hearing each other over the drawl that emanated from the large speakers.

At one point, I went to the room with the plumbing to syphon the python, leaving the attractive young woman alone at the bar whilst doing so, and returned to find the young woman in question being leered over by one of those burly, tight-shirt-wearing, shitty-haircut douchebags. I approached the situation calmly at first, but the dickhead got smart, and indignance in the eye of the savage beast is something I cannot walk away from. I stood straight and gallant, but physics are physics, and he and his friends were bigger than me. I got pushed around a bit and then security dealt with the fuckers, leaving Sandra and I none the worse for wear and with a free drink each for our troubles. So, all in all, a productive expenditure of energy.

We left shortly thereafter and found the brutes outside, surrounded by a surprising quantity of pigs. We snuck the scene.

I got the impression that she had liked my playing the macho role and defending her honour, because she was smirking over at me all the way back to my place.

'*So, this is where Eddy Sky kicks up his feet at the end of the day,*' she observed as I flicked on the light.

'*I guess it is.*'

I went to my kitchenette and fixed her a drink, because that's what grown-ups do.

'*Eddy?*'

'*Yes.*'

'*Do you think we're doing a good thing? At work, I mean.*'

I turned and handed her the drink. She was on my couch, half sprawled, with her arms spread across the length of the back section, one leg folded over the other, and her head tilted questioningly. The pose would have made her look sexy if she were wearing a nice dress and some makeup, but as it were, with her bare face and T-shirt and jeans, she just looked very cute.

My normal reaction to such a question would've probably been, '*I don't know and I don't care,*' but given my recent foray into soft contentedness, as well as the fact that she happened to be carrying the key to my happiness comfortably in her pants, I was all too willing to play along.

'*Well, it is what it is. If we didn't do it, someone else would do it worse.*'

I fired up my brand-new stereo system (an expensive present for myself, see the above mention of soft contentedness) and put on *Coltrane*.

'*I guess,*' she replied.

I sat next to her.

'*Think of it this way. People should be free to do what they want, right?*'

'*Right.*'

'*So, we're just giving them the option. They don't HAVE to get high, but if they WANT to, they can, thanks to us.*'

She nodded. '*You're right. I just think about stuff sometimes, you know?*'

What a terrible phrase.

'*I thought you didn't want to talk about work tonight,*' I diverted, my best smirk on display.

She smiled back. '*I did say that, didn't I?*'

'Yes, ma'am.'

'Should we do something else, then?'

Wowsa! Not even two sips into my scotch, not even halfway through *Equinox*, and already things were heating up in Sky Manor. But before I could go in for the kiss, she turned away and started going through her tiny handbag. Again, it took a while to find what she was looking for, but eventually she pulled out a small baggie of white powder. I had done *kiddy coke* before, but never the grown-ups' stuff; that was a rich man's drug.

'Do you wanna?' she asked, already pouring the contents onto my coffee table.

Ladies and gentlemen, I did.

She cut a generous line for me using her Medicare card (whac-ka-whacka) and then one for herself, then we snorted simultaneously.

Let me tell you something, friends. Whoever was the sage poet that coined the phrase *'Don't get high on your own supply'* had obviously never been privy to the supply of *Sunbeam Solutions*. That is to say, it was good shit.

We began to make out enthusiastically, and that *Bob Dylan* tune started up in my head, the first track off *Blonde on Blonde* (figure it out); a fitting soundtrack considering how awkward a job I thought I was doing.

We migrated over to the bed and the clothes came off. I marvelled at how large her areolas were, also how much pussy hair she was sporting; the latter was a slight turnoff, but beggars can't be choosers.

When she sat on my dick, I thought I was going to cum straight up, due to both my excitement and the unexpected warmth, but she sensed my sensitivity and moved slowly.

I didn't wear a condom (presuming a modern woman like her would be on the pill) and it had been a few days since the little Asian lady with the bad breath had beat me hard and sore, so my cock was nice and fresh and receptive.

Being of the dirty age of internet pornography, I pulled out when the urge came and spurted on her face. To my slight surprise, she wasn't crazy about this, but she washed up and stayed the night anyway.

There was more coke and round two later, and then coffee and round three the next morning. It was nice and all, but I was mainly just happy to have it over with; the popping of my virtuous cherry.

When she left, I lay a while in the bed that now smelled of her; essential oils and natural shampoo. I thought about the oboe-playing cunt next door, hoping that we had kept him up a bit. It felt good to be the noisy one for once. It felt good to be a grown-up.

CHAPTER EIGHT

'*Shut up. Shut the fuck up!*' I screamed at the wall, the sound bouncing back into my own ears more than it penetrated through.

'*Bite me,*' Replied the nasal, indignant little voice.

I had only seen the voice's owner once; some ineffective little four-eyes cunt who would have looked just as out of place on any respectable bandstand as the instrument he played.

Let me set the scene for y'all fucking moderates. I had come home after a long day at work, having had to deal with some thieving little shit that afternoon, to the not-so-dulcet tones of some airy-fairy shit from the oboe next door. What a drag-and-a-half.

'*Learn some decent music, at least. Fuck!*'

'*You know nothing of decent music, Mr. Coltrane, Mr. Bojangles.*'

'*Eat shit! Eat my shit!*' I roared. "*If you don't shut your goddamn lips in the next ten-seconds, I'm going to kick in your door and shit down your sound hole, motherfucker, see if it seeps through to the reeve.*'

There was silence for several seconds, and I thought I had bested him. But then he started up again, twice as loud as before and wildly atonal, obviously to spite me.

I stormed toward the door in long strides. It was a happy coincidence that I needed to take a shit anyway, and so I fully intended to follow through with my promise.

I opened the door to find my landlord, a greying old fool named Ron, standing outside and looking at me pityingly. I didn't know at the time that the oboist was Ron's son, and on account of my getting into a loud argument with the mailman the week before, my tenancy was a flimsy little thing to begin with.

And with that, it was goodbye, Mr. Sky. Not so nice knowing you, and don't you dare slam the door on your way out.

I gathered my only possessions – my clothes, my bottle of Chivas, and my stereo – and walked out of that shitty blue building for the last time.

Sandra was sitting on her front verandah, smoking a cigarette and off in some absent world. She didn't see my Uber roll up and she didn't see me push open the front gate. It wasn't until my heavy Doc Martens (don't say a fucking word) thudded against the bottom step that she snapped to and stood to greet me. I'd forgotten to tell her I was coming; everything had happened too quickly. One moment I had my own pad, the next I did not. My bubble of complacent contentedness had been shaken, though unfortunately not popped.

I saw her noticing my stuff. She frowned.

'What happened?'

'I got kicked out of my place.'

'Shit, that's a bummer,' she replied.

It had only been three weeks since our first date, but things were moving along steadily. We had spent many a night at my place, and not *just* fucking like stoned rabbits, either, actually talking a bit as well. I had known that I liked her very much, but it wasn't until that moment, standing at the bottom of the stairs with my suitcase and my stereo, that I realised I was in love with her. What had pushed me over the edge was her reaction to the eviction news. She hadn't asked *'Why?'* or *'What did you do?'* she had accepted the situation and offered sympathy, no forlorn comments or needling.

I came up the stairs, put down my stuff, and kissed her. Apologies for the sappy romantic shit, but I'm just telling you what happened. It felt good to have someone to go to, someone who would take me in, and though I was aware this was a complacent emotion and I was losing my edge on account of it, I didn't care in that moment.

'What a sorry fucking sight. A man with his life in a suitcase.'

I broke our hug and looked over at Sunny, who had just emerged from inside. He was dressed in his usual night-out outfit: Ripped jeans, no shoes, rose glasses. His lanky six-foot-two arse came over and forced us into a three-way hug.

'You can stay here as long as you need. I sleepwalk naked and erect, but if that doesn't bother you, me casa you casa, cunt.'

And with that, he kissed me on my pretty little head and walked on down the street.

'He was joking, right?' I asked as Sandra led me inside.

'It's a two-thirds truth,' she replied without elaborating further.

We went into her room and she began to make a spot for me in her big wardrobe. I sat on the bed and clasped my hands, the drag of the situation subsiding some.

It wasn't so much that I was stressed about the sudden eviction; I was more stressed about having to ask someone for help. I probably could have swindled myself some other form of accommodation, but only just. As generous as I thought my weekly wage (having now increased to $1000), and as far as it would seem to go in my mind, I always managed to piss it away somehow.

Sandra gave me a Valium to calm my nerves. I dry swallowed and started to feel better.

In the wee hours, during a jaunt to the bathroom, I discovered which of the two-thirds were true. There was Sunny, sleepwalking and naked, but ultimately flaccid.

'I love Glen Ford, but he ain't no Santa Claus,' he mumbled.

'Go back to bed, you weirdo,' I replied.

There was a long pause.

'Okay,' he said, before letting out one big snore and walking away.

This was my new home.

That morning I was called into Sunny's office. He sat there behind his big, important desk, eating cereal messily and wearing nothing but socks.

I remembered a book my father had kept on his bookshelf. It was called *The Naked CEO*. I thought that maybe Sunbeam had read this book and taken it a little too literally (cha-cha-cha).

'Who the fuck is Glen Ford?' I enquired, slumping into the chair.

'Never heard of him,' he replied. He seemed impatient, tired, barely interested in his usual circuitous nature. *'Eddy, it's time.'*

Finally, fuck. For weeks, there had been something going on in the office, something big. Being the needling type, I had often tried to squeeze the information out of Sunny's Rasta-like head, but he never budged. His retort to my incessancy was always the same: *'You will be brought in when the time is right, and no sooner.'*

Well, apparently the time was upon us. Hurray for unfolding secrets.

'There's a deal in the works. Some big-time underground types from Sydney want to buy us out.'

'Fuck that,' I replied.

'Well ...' He stopped. I waited for him to go on, but apparently he had nothing more to say.

I was averse to the idea, not because I had formed any sort of emotional connection to the business or to Sunny himself, but damned if I hadn't to Sandra, and they both meant something to her. Plus, there was the matter of the cash influx I might lose. Once you get a taste of the sweet crotch of capitalism, it's much easier to keep your teeth sunk into its velvety flesh than to walk away from it.

'So that's it, huh?'

'There's still the finer points to be worked on, we're still in the early stages. I'm telling you now because we're meeting with them for the first time next week.'

'We? Fucking hell, why do I have to be there?'

'Because of your charm and knowledge of the day-to-day.'

'You know the day-to-day stuff as well as I do.'

'But I don't have your charm,' he replied, irritated.

'*Just remember to put on clothes and you'll be fine.*'

'*Yes, that's another thing. I want you to wear a suit.*'

'I don't own a suit ... and I'm not going, anyway.'

His eyes flashed with anger, but he took a deep breath and managed to control himself. '*I need you with me on this one. I'll give you some money, and you and Sandra can go suit shopping. It will be like one of those romantic montages in the movies.*'

'*Those movies are shit,*' I barked rebelliously.

This was when he snapped.

'*And so are you, shit heel! And you'd better get some new shoes as well, those Docs make you look like fucking K.D. Lang!*'

'*K.D. LANG DOESN'T WEAR SHOES!*' I screamed.

'*FUCKING ELLEN DEGENERES, THEN!*'

I exploded to my feet and with one angry swipe of my outstretched arm, cleared the large desk of all that stood thereon. Papers and his many small ornaments went flying.

'*YOU LITTLE SHIT!*' he growled.

He came at me from around the desk with some odd, dancing stance. I started laughing, I couldn't help it, but then he knocked me into yesterday with a few swift movements, and I wasn't laughing anymore. Wouldn't you believe it that the lanky hippy, who walked around naked and pretty much had two left feet, was a fucking Capoeira master?

I got up and saw that he was laughing, and you know what? I started laughing again too. Maybe I *had* taken a shine to dear old Sunbeam River, after all. This was a fight between friends.

'*O-okay,*' he said between walloping giggles. '*Free shot, and then back to work.*'

He spread out his arms and closed his eyes. I was more or less in hysterics as I wound back my fist and walked towards my boss, but just as I was about to even the score ...

'*What the fuck!*'

It was Sandra, having heard the commotion and opened the door on the strange occasion. I turned and saw her react to my face. I shot her a bloody smile.

'*What's happening?*' she asked as her fellow office girls and two of the guys from phone repair crowded the door.

'*Sunny insulted my footwear.*'

This instigated a fresh wave of laughter between him and I.

'*H-h-hey, Eddy,*' Sunny said.

I turned to face him again. He hit himself on the cheek harder than I would have thought it possible for anyone to hit themselves, then fell to the floor.

The rest of the day was somewhat normal, and that night Sunny and I had a fire engine on the back deck and bonded over the fight. I agreed to come to the meeting.

CHAPTER NINE

And so, there was your dear pal Eddy Sky, dressed in a five-hundred-dollar suit and a spanking new pair of shoes.

The shopping expedition with Sandra had been somewhat more bearable than expected (that is to say, she blew me in the changing room), and I'll begrudgingly admit that it felt good to wear the garments in question. I felt clean and important.

I was waiting in the front room of Sunbeam Estate under a blaring ceiling fan and the watchful eyes of the tropical fishies in the corner. *Back and forth.*

Sandra had explained to me that morning that I often came across as confrontational (duh) and petulant (false) and gave me a Valium so that I might level out. But at about the time the windowpanes started melting out of their frames, I started to think maybe the little pill she had given me was something other than Valium, and when a certain clownfish with a Jamaican accent winked in my direction and told me to only drink Mount Franklin (*'Hey, Eddy man! Are you gonna tell me I don't know water?'*), I was almost sure of it.

I laid myself on the white couch and hugged my cocoon, hoping the world would reassert itself at some future point, preferably soon. In swam Sunny River in his best suit and his fogged-up rose speccers.

'Looking sharp, Mr. Sky,' said his bubbles as they popped by my ears, leaving in their taste a big *WWOOOOOSSSSSHHHHH! WWAAAAAAAAS-SHHHHH!* as I fell to our great celestial, and there was my friend on the cloud beside me.

'Are you okay?' he yelled through his beak, struggling to be heard over the *WWOOOOOOSSSSSHHHHH!*

'Sandra gave me sustenance for my confrontational tendencies!'

'What? Why are you yelling?' he yelled back before letting out a resounding, *SQUUAAAAAAAACCCCCKKKK!*

Then the misfortune to realise crested his expression.

'Oh, shit ...' was his last dear whisper before we hit the ground, and then came the white.

The room faded back into focus. I slapped together my thumb and pointer finger a few times, my go-to when deciphering if shit has hit; they felt springy, which was a yes sir.

Sunny knelt by my front and held my (face) cheeks tenderly.

'Eddy, you're on drugs.'

'I'd fucking hope so,' I replied.

'We need to get you to bed.'

He tried to hoist my petite frame. I didn't *mean* to resist, but my limpness was a foremost travesty.

'It was just a vitamin-V, I'm tripping the fuck out.'

'It was a vitamin-V coated in acid, a new invention of mine.'

'Youfuckingpsychopathyou'reagenius,' I think I said aloud.

There was a knock at the front door, a courtesy one as the cunt was already ajar (it's not a jar, it's a door, yuk-yuk-yuk). On the doorway vestibule was a group of five penguins who varied in age but were all tanned douchebags.

At first I thought they were some new corporate-drone types come to get their jollies (they would often show up before or after work to fill their pretty little baskets), but when Sunny-beamy greeted them with a concerted effort to hide his inherent awkwardness, I realised they must be the buyers.

I was slumped on the couch, having been dropped onto it after the lanky Rasta man had run to the feet of his new masters.

'What's wrong with him?' pointed the lead suit after Sunny's attempt to distract them with formalities had failed.

'Eddy Sky, good sir. Shake my hand and be my man,' I blurted whilst springing from my pile and striding to the crown.

I thought he stood a little straighter during our firm handshake; this was a good sign. I stood there next to my boss, hoping it was the world that was swaying and not I.

The crowd was nondescript in their likeness, all the dogdamned same, to put it crudely, except for a short Asian man with glasses who hung behind his friends and had a huge dick on his forehead.

We began with the standard business drivel that is no different in its form whether it take place in a boardroom among meek, or in the hallway of a drug house among hooligans. This masquerade was followed by a tour.

I added my charming little quips and operational summaries, but it was all fairly drab, as I had been suddenly overcome by an urge to go ice fishing out on Lake Wivenhoe and wanted these pricks to leave so I could catch the bus out there and do so. I'd have to go buy a rod first, but that was an easy detour.

As I was trying to figure out how I would go about cutting a hole in the ice, I was rudely interrupted by the brutish leader.

'Do they ever give you grief, Eddy?'

I snapped to and realised we were in the mail room. He was referring to my beloved process labourers.

'Oh, no, Hal.' I addressed the domed red light on his forehead.

'They are nothing less than model citizens.'

This got a laugh – when surrounded by idiots, you can say anything in a well tone and get a laugh. Still, their affirmation gave me cheap warmth.

Next stop was the nerd den (phone repair room), which I was technically responsible for but did my best to avoid due to its lack of natural light depressing me. I had to divert all the technical questions in its relation to Alex (lead repair man) and he helped me out with the nitty-gritty.

If not for the calm pill in my digestive, I probably would have brained the Marshmallow Man when we went into the office and he put his big, gooey hands on the sweet, rounded shoulders of my beloved and made an untoward comment about wanting to thoroughly go over her books, but I just laughed it off and called him a big, white cunt and all went over well.

At the tour's conclusion, the four-eyes with the droopy dick and the Hal-9000 man were escorted into Sunny's office to discuss finance and other boring shit while I was left in the reception area to entertain the other three gentlemen.

They asked me all sorts of garrulous questions I didn't know the answers to (What's the best strip joint? How far to the Gold Coast?) but I managed as best I could, given the circumstances.

Then there were some more formalities, then it was goodbye Mr/s Sky and Water. Apparently, they had some other important shit to do (a circle jerk, for all I cared) and went on their merry way. They would be back here and there throughout the next few days, but I would then be better equipped to deal with their bore.

Sunny looked at me and sighed as their car sped away. *'You did good,'* he told me.

'Whatever you say, sellout. Just don't put all your eggs in one conglomerate pouch ... cunt face.'

The rest of the day was filled with my sleeping it off in the sweet-smelling linen of Sandra's bed. I had some interesting dreams and soliloquies in waking – including the tender and mine BB coming in to apologise for giving me the wrong pill (not sure whether dream or soliloquy) – and by that night the toxins had mainly left me alone, though I did wonder, on account of it being a full moon, if I was turning into a werewolf.

CHAPTER TEN

By the end of the week, the deal had been finalised and I could finally go about my duties without the constant and moronic interjections of the brutes in suits. They had gone back to Sydney for a week while they finalised all the stuff on their end. They would then send back the happy folk who were – after a transitory period of two weeks during which the current staff would work alongside them – to inherit the kingdom.

Sunny had initially been flaky about revealing the amount settled for, but after much of my trademark pestering, he eventually caved and told me (probably looking down and to the left when he said it) that the number was $100,000. I thought at the time it sounded like a logical amount. The funny thing about growing up as a spoiled rich kid is that you never learn to question the value of money, and so – as an adult – when someone tells you that $100,000 is a large quantity of the stuff, you believe them. It may seem a contradiction, but it's actually entirely logical; being socially sheltered (by way of ingrained snobbishness and superiority) and well-fed happens to be the perfect recipe for a person to not question the economics of things. So yes, $100,000 seemed a logical amount.

He also told me I would get five percent to compensate for my loss of employment. Not bad. Fucking terrific, in fact. Eddy Sky was about to become a rich young man. Maybe I could buy one of those old-fashioned coffee carts and wheel it from place to place, pollute the callow with a legal drug for once. What a sorry sight that would be.

I loathed the buyers and felt sorry for Sunny, downtrodden as he was about it all, but there was nothing I could do. The business world in general is a bad enough place, and I did what I could to live outside of it. But the more specific realm of corporate acquirement is another evil entirely; a long-fanged, rabid beast that only the most naïve and ignorant of cunts don't know to stay away from. As much as I was fond of Sunny, I wasn't about to stand between him and the impending savagery.

My personal life that week was an even more tumultuous affair. Something I have neglected to mention thus far is that dearest Sandra was one itchy mumma. Apart from (and in part of) her consistent intake of chemical inebriates, her sexual appetite was more or less insatiable.

We started out taking stuff together. Uppers or downers, it didn't matter. We just wanted to feel what it was like to leave our genitals entangled on the ground and float our heads up in the sky. But then she had the idea that we could both take a different substance each, and that wasn't so grand.

I remember one occasion when I was laying peacefully on her bed, wrapped in a perfect cocoon of wine and Mother's Little Helper (uncoated this time), and in she came all worked up on coke and almost tore the stitching out of my jeans because she wanted to do her next line off my erect penis. It might have been a fun experience, all things being equal, but I only owned a few pairs of pants and didn't want to have to go shopping for more.

Another night, after an MDMA vs. Ludes affair, she asked me what I thought it would be like to take heroin together. I'd never taken the grandest junk and didn't really have any interest in doing so, so I brushed off the question with my usual charm and tact, but it did worry me. Perhaps her casually fuck-uppery wasn't such a casual thing after all.

My favourite times with her were when we were sober – or as sober as Sandra (the walking medicine cabinet of madness) ever was. But even then, she never seemed all that satisfied after. It was almost as if (actually, it was *definitely* the case) my dear lady simply saw no point in having sex whilst sober. Sex to her was an exploration of the self, a journey into the inner realms of her own altered mind. It had nothing to do with the *us* of it all. This really got to me.

On Tuesday night, as I was undergoing my *crucial* daily self-reflection period, she burst into the bedroom with the wildest eyes I had ever seen in her pretty little head. Is it possible for the word *'rejuvenated'* to be meant as a pejorative? Well, that's how it was. The sex was anxious and selfish, more so than usual, and she absolutely insisted that I cum in her mouth, beating my meat hard and dry (reminding me of the good old days of the massage parlour) to make it so, like a perverted, cum-ravenous zombie.

She was quiet the next morning, and I let her sulk around for a bit, but upon confronting her later she told me that last night she'd shot up. There it was, the Big n' Dirty. My beloved had finally graduated from kiddy school.

She was adamant that she would remain clean of *any* substances for the rest of the day, but just as the sun was going down, I caught her blazing a joint.

'Don't judge me, motherfucker,' was her defence.

Later that night, as we lay happily in her big, fragrant bed, she quite casually instigated a conversation on the subject of non-monogamy. More specifically, our potential to foray into it. More specifically still, *her* potential to foray into it.

'You can watch ... if you want,' she had said.

I promptly called her a whore and left to find a hotel. She'd made similar hints in the past, but I had never taken it seriously; blinded by the love-induced rushes of blood to my heart and dick, I must have missed many things. What a drag – my girlfriend was a heartless cunt and I wasn't good enough for her. May as well be dragged through dog shit.

I woke up in a lavish ninth-floor hotel room the next morning and texted Sunny to say that I wasn't coming in to work, then threw my phone out the window. It was just a burner.

I yearned for the device to crack the feeble skull of a so-deserving passer-by, some giddy entrepreneur in a perfect world, but unfortunately, I heard no scream from below, so I went and checked out instead.

I walked around the city for a bit, enjoying my morning off, then retired to some la-di-da joint for a breakfast of pancakes and scrambled on toast and also some glorious bacon – just to spite the vegan shrew I had previously loved (not that she had any way of knowing). I had plenty of cashola in my tight little pockets, but when the time came to pay the piper, I decided to dash anyway. A little thrill to keep the pulp in my noggin amused.

I thought about swiping some hard liquid from whatever juice joint I next came upon, but then what? I'd end up drinking it in the daylight, having no good place to make myself exclusive. A great sadness of living in the city is seeing the drunks with no home but the gutter, all filthy and crazy, easy pickings for the pigs. I didn't want to be like them. What an old, ineffective cunt I was becoming – hesitant against my basic instinct to steal.

I went and bought a coffee instead, just to spite the green tea-loving shrew with whom I had, up until recently, made a habit of exchanging bodily fluids (not that she had any way of knowing, and what an irony to drink green tea in the morning and shoot heroin at night).

That afternoon I went into The Valley and hit up my old favourite rub-and-tug-factory ('Hi, darling. Me miss you for long!'). Her prices had gone up, but I didn't make a fuss. Times were tough, and apparently even the working girls were feeling sore (whacka-whacka).

By the beginning of that night, I ashamedly began to miss my unabashed little minx, and the terrible truth is that my sweet, innocent eyes dropped a tear for the way she was. Against my better intellect, I ended up back at the house – hence completing the first natural cycle of our breakups and makeups.

The second of our breakups and makeups began when I woke up the next morning and realised the perils of my emotional weakness. I felt like an insipid little man, even more so than my physical state of five-foot-nine would have you believe. I still instigated a little morning-delight sober session, but I came intentionally quickly in an attempt to get back at her and then told her we were through just as the last waves of pleasure were subsiding.

We worked together bitterly the rest of the morning, and when the office gathered for lunch – pumpkin soup – she almost threw my bowl at me, and there happened to be a big ol' loogie floating within.

When the factory whistle rang at five o'clock, I swung my jacket over my shoulder and whistled my way out into the kitchen, where I met her gaze from across the floating island. We both stopped dead at the sight of the other and adopted a sourpuss each, and there we stood like a god-damned stand off until the absurdity of the situation hit us and we both burst into laughter. We made up that night using methods you can proba-bly guess at yourself. This was Thursday.

Friday was uneventful and the weekend was the same. Monday, on the other hand, was when shit really flew up in the air, and as I have already described the state of the ceiling fans in Sunbeam Estate, I'm sure you can imagine what happened when it got there.

The whole fucking dance began when the Sydney boys walked in sport-ing their neatly pressed suits, their inarticulate neck tattoos peeking out from underneath their unfortunately loose collars. Among the crowd were Hal-9000 and the Dickhead, as well the Marshmallow Man douchebag who had hit on Sandra. They walked in without knocking, as if they owned the place (hah-hah) and wasted no time in making a list of the things they planned to change during the transitory period and beyond. The first thing they coup'd against was the grand downward draft that swelled all around and rustled their rooster cuts so. I looked over at Sunny as they flipped the knob to the *off* position, closed the front door, and began to fiddle with the dusty air-con remote, but he just shrugged. Fucking great, I'd be spending the next two weeks in a hermetically sealed, toxic-aired, Lynx-Africa-smelling ode to an empire that was. I bet they'd be shunning Sandra's beautiful home-cooked lunches in favour of McDonald's and pro-tein shakes as well.

I must have developed something akin to pride for our little opera-tion, because each time our new masters added a *'change item'* to their list, I died inside just a little bit. The mail room was to be reformatted to both '*improve productivity*' and allow for a more '*streamlined*' sorting process. The happy workers I had once supervised were apprehensive of the intruders, but loosened up when Hal-9000 addressed them and assured they would not be losing their jobs. They then became bemused and angry when he went on to say they would be made to strip naked and don plastic body suits '*to avoid contamination*'. Obviously bullshit; theft is the allegory.

Sunny was quiet as a mouse during Hal's speech, stoic as Aurelius and watching the pink floor.

The phone-repair aspect was to be liquidated, but Alex would be retained in another capacity, seeming as it did that the Dickhead had taken a shine to him for some reason and needed an assistant. I later found out that Alex had been studying finance in his spare time, so the appointment made sense.

I was mildly surprised by their lack of interest in the phone stuff, but I guess they had their own legitimate operations; funnels and diversions.

Sunny had once explained to me the importance of the phone business.

'*The trick is that I declare all our income as legitimate through the phone cover. That way, if I ever get caught, at least I'll have paid tax on everything. Could be a difference of years in the clink. People don't care as much about corrupted children as they do stolen money.*'

The man in question had been reduced to a shell in a suit by mid-morning, his forlorn face a stark contrast to his pink glasses and ridiculous floral tie.

Upon our entering the office, the fucking Marshmallow Man shot my sweetheart a smile that I didn't like one bit, and I swear I saw a slight bulge appear in his pants as well. She smiled back non-offensively enough, but maintained eye contact just a moment too long. I planned to break up with her for good at the end of the transitory period, but I felt a jealous stab just the same.

All the office girls were destined to bite the dust when the regime proper commenced. But they knew this – had known for the past week and a half – so Hal's address to them was met with a resounding ho-hum.

Half a dozen more Sydney suits arrived at midday, none of them looking even mildly capable of thought, and wasted no time in getting off their tits on coke and jumping around the coolly conditioned walls.

The new higher-level fools decided to nip at the feet of the current higher-level fucks in a fleeting attempt at education; that is to say, Sunny was showing Hal and some other cunt (probably Hal's assistant – he looked like the subservient, bottom-feeder type) the ropes while Sandra took care of the Dickhead and Alex, and I took care of some square-faced prick named Tyrone who would be taking over my incredulous reins.

Despite his brutish appearance, Tyrone was quiet and polite, and he listened when he had to and asked questions when that was the pertinent thing to do, so I liked him okay.

We spent the early afternoon in the mail room, going over shit and fucking about a bit, then when 3 pm came, we made our way to the front reception/makeshift circle jerk area (in which they had set up some overflow desks where a bunch of lower-levels were working) to kindly greet our grommet afterschool streetwalkers, collect their earnings, and refill their cute little pockets.

Now, I loathed the fact that most of the Sydney cunts had moronic nicknames for each other, but Tyrone's affectionate *'Psycho-T'* had piqued my interest since he seemed such a calm and subdued young man. I was lucky enough to see Psycho-T roar to life with a resounding *'WHAT THE FUCK!'* when one of our little Eshays came in and sheepishly told me that he was fifty bucks short. I was getting ready to give him a stern talking-to and send him on his merry way when Tyrone pushed me to the ground (myself being an obstruction between him and the kid), screamed the aforementioned phrase, and punched him in the chest so hard that I thought for a second it might've stopped his heart. The kid ran out yelping, and Sunny burst out of his office to check on the commotion.

'Sorry, Eddy,' said the subsiding Psycho-T alter ego, helping me to my feet.

'What the fuck was that about?' asked Sunny, rushing over to watch the kid run. He then slammed the door and turned angrily to Tyrone.

Hal walked over and put a hand on Sunny's shoulder.

'Easy fella, it's an emotional business.'

'You want the whole fucking street to hear shit like that?'

Hal nodded and hid his smile. *'You're right. Watch yourself, T. Save the big stuff for when we've got the soundproofing and blocked out the windows.'*

There were other such 'emotional' displays throughout the day, an angry phone call here and a disillusioned process worker there, and it all amounted to my increasing and dangerous scorn. I had watched Sunny's face drop by the hour, such a sorry sight indeed, and at knockoff time, he limped out defeatedly to his nightly *rendezvous* with a series of bars and bland beverages.

The new boys left as well, some to drink and harass girls daring enough to wear low and/or tight skirts, some back to their hotels – or maybe they had permanent accommodation by then, I don't fucking know nor care – leaving Sandra and I alone at the house. We sat on the back deck, smoking cigarettes and discussing our day like a regular old pair of co-dependant fools and taking in the seasonably warm early evening and the pleasant din of cicadas.

'What do you think's gonna happen when it's over?' she asked me in her dreamy way. She had been a nostalgic little sprite around that time, amongst all her regular ups and downs.

'I don't know, I guess I'll get a real job. Work in a bookstore or something.'

She laughed at me a little. *'I can't imagine you in retail.'*

'What the fuck does it matter? It's either that, or …' I struggled to find the right words and shortly gave up.

'I think I'm gonna move to the country, somewhere quiet. Find a regional uni to transfer to,' said she.

There was a long pause. I watched her starry eyes as they looked out over the sea of square backyards enveloped in the now-familiar haze. I had loved those eyes, very much so, but now they just made me tired.

'... You can come with me, if you want.'

It was all there in the wording; not *'I want you to'*, not even *'Would you like to?'*, but *'If you want.'* She'd used the same syntax with the non-monogamy shit. What it really meant was, *'I don't want you to, but I'm trying to be polite about it. Do please pick up on this particular subtlety.'*

I was beyond scolding her. It had all become such an effort. But then ...

'I want you to,' was what she sighed.

Well, well. I'll be dipped in septic and licked clean thereafter; I was wrong. I guess it was the thing in her face – that same, ingrained *thing* that gave her the vacant smile; her casual, charming disconnect – that also made it hard for her to speak as she really felt.

She turned and looked at me. *'I want you to, Eddy.'*

'I ... Don't. Know. How I feel, Sandy ...' And it wasn't a lie. I thought I'd known, mere seconds ago I was sure of it, but now, with her big smiling eyes there in front of me, straight up asking if I would build a life with her ... fuck, dude.

I saw the disappointment in her face, I guess my uncertainty was answer enough, and she turned away. Funny, I always thought I'd been the most in love, but maybe it had been her. But then, why had she been so troubled by the prospect of making love with a clear mind? Fuck knows. The day I understand the heart of a woman will be the day I see the universe. Apologies for the sappy shit again – I'm quite the fucking poet at times – but what's the damage; we write what we write and then we die.

'Will you think about it?' she asked, hoping against her apparent instinct.

'Did I ever tell you about Lauren Grace?'

I have no idea where it came from (you douchebag literary and psychoanalytical cunts can try to figure it out, if you'd like), but it seemed important to tell her.

'No,' she answered.

'A girl from school, real smart and pretty and a good egg.'

'Then what?'

'Then I found her tied to a tree with her guts hanging out. She wasn't so pretty then.' (Ba-dum tsss ...)

'Huh,' she replied thoughtfully, probably thinking I was either speaking in metaphor or making some crass joke about impermanence.

'Yea, I'll think about it,' I lied.

She made her way to the underside of my arm. The night was beautiful, but none for me. Only bittersweet.

'There's something I need to tell you,' she said after a while.

'Do I really need to hear it?'

'Yes.'

She straightened herself so that she could look into my face. I had to endure many half-exhalations as she went to start but stopped at the last. Finally, she blurted, *'You're being ripped off, dude. I know you never look at the books, but c'mon! That five percent of a hundred grand – do you really think all this is only worth a hundred grand? And your wage, I mean ...'*

I held up a hand, signalling her to stop, and took a moment to process this. Now, it's a tough thing for a man to be confronted by his own ignorance, and I bet you think I flew into a rage, but you may be proud to know I was able to control myself. Instead, I took her back under my arm and tried to forget about it and enjoy her presence. I was angry, yes – Sunny was a piece o' shit, shim-sham man all right, and I a foolish boy for not realising from the start. I was also angry at Sandra, more so for loving me than for not telling me sooner – but my anger was impotent. I could've simply gone about the business of beating the living shit out of her brother if I *didn't* love her, but I *did,* and therefore I was impotent. Gan and Sartre, curse this beating heart.

The following morning was when I woke up next to her for the very last time. We'd just drank some wine the night before, so nothing too crazy transpired after the clothes left our bodies, but it was a nice goodbye. I gathered my stereo and my clothes and slipped away before she woke.

Coda

CHAPTER ELEVEN

The fools that surround me, I tell you.

There I was, back in the rat hole – my old boarding house in South Bank. A few shekels a night for room and board and all the lead-based paint chips you could eat. I missed my place on Albert Street. I even missed the kid with the oboe; he hadn't been so bad in hindsight. It was me being the loud neighbour these days.

I was lying in my little room, my fancy-pants stereo blasting some *Townes Van Zandt*, and all these dickheads in the adjoining rooms were yelling out angry incoherencies and completely ruining the experience. It had been a tiring afternoon of walking around & waiting for something to happen, and all I wanted was to veg out a bit, but noooooo.

BOOM. BOOM. BOOM, went the paper-thin wall.

'*SHUT THE FUCK UP! I'LL KILL YA, YOU LITTLE SHIT!*' spat one of my charming neighbours.

Ain't the city a grand old place? It was my third death threat that week, though it probably didn't help that I lived amongst a bunch of ex-cons.

'*FUCK YOUR ANGER AND FUCK YOUR MOTHER!*' I replied. How dare he disrupt my *critical* meditation period.

The prick didn't reply, and I thought for a second he might be heading over to kick in my door, but no.

It had been a week since I'd walked out of the River household for the last time, and not one call or text had I made or received. This was good. There would be a time to collect my five grand, of course. Maybe even squeeze out a bit more for my anguish, but that time was not now.

BANG!

Fucking hell – a fist through my wall, then an angry eye looking in through the newly made hole.

'*I swear to god, if you don't shut that country shit off!*' said the eye. Some other of my charming neighbours voiced their agreement.

'*Fine!*' I replied, reaching for my headphones. '*But if you speak a negative word of my music ever again, I'll shit in your pillowcase, mate.*'

I plugged them in and the ignorant eye went away. A lot of my threats centred around shitting in or on something, and I laughed aloud as I realised this for the first time.

I had no plans for the future, nor vague aspirations, but fuck it all; eighteen is a time for having fun and scrapping in dirt. It was all a regrettable and unavoidable shit-show, my happy and impulsive existence, my fleeting '*youth*' and impending irrelevance. What is ageing if not the gradual decline of everything that is good? But at least I had a life at all; poor Lauren.

James MacMillan had presented his sorry and crooked mug in front of a judge and crown prosecutor that morning, as I had been informed by a reliable source. Apparently, he had wept uncontrollably when the powers that govern found probable *mens rea* and *actus reus*.

The murder had occurred on the eve of his eighteenth birthday at approximately 10:35 pm. The cunt had called up poor Lauren and asked her for an early birthday present (a good, hard fuck, you see). She had initially refused, but changed her mind when James dangled the sweet carrot of a few hundred bucks in front of her hungry little rabbit nose. He had driven her to the top of Glen Rock, taken her into the bush, killed her, raped her, then went home and became a man. But here's the kicker, ladies and gentlemen. Despite the judge acknowledging the gravity of the crime, and that the perpetrator was mere hours from being of legal age, he still decided to convict James as a minor, and so the punishment for the slaying of Lauren Grace was a two-year stint in a youth correctional facility followed by three years on parole. That's right, folks. That's the price of a life in our great society.

It's funny, though: two years *did* seem like a long time back then. I didn't know how the years would fly by – even my early twenties seemed an obscure concept – but even if someone had told me so, I probably wouldn't have listened.

I lay there on my dirty floor in the tiny room I shared with rats and cockroaches and mildew, with asbestos that rained from the ceiling in plumes if you slammed the door too hard, and thought about all this, and I realised that, against all reason and evidence, I was a happy young man. Even a tired, old roof that looked as if it might collapse at any moment was better than the fancy, pressed tin I had lived under with my loving parents. I had come a long way. I was also happy because I knew that everything could change in an instant; such is the potential of living impulsively in this simultaneous world.

I hope that, in reading this account, you have not come to be afraid, pitiful, or empathetic of me. I don't want your emotions. Near the beginning of this extended tirade, I told you in no uncertain terms that the reason I steal shit is because I believe no one can own anything, and I still think this way, but I would like to add a second reason: I also steal because I am better than you. So, if you ever see me climbing in through your bathroom window late one night, or maybe running out of your local liquor store with a case of beer under each arm, don't be so quick to call on the services of your local police force. Instead, remember this: **<u>rules are for idiots</u>.**

CHAPTER TWELVE

And wouldn't that have been a humdinger of a note to end on. But alas, there is one more thing I would like to tell you about. It won't take long.

That Friday night, I took the crosstown bus over to grand old Paddington, and on the way, something interesting happened. There was I, trundling along Coronation Drive in the company of my fellow passengers, keeping to myself and thinking my thoughts. The bus's overhead lights were not flickering, the moon was not full, the stars were not many, the night was most certainly not sultry, and yet – in a world so full of absences – there was *something*. We stopped at a red light and I looked down at the river, which reflected nothing. Standing at the edge and looking into it was a lone dingo. That's right, folks – a dingo in the city, an impossible sight if ever I've seen one. That dingo was free. Not because it was alone, but because it saw absence where the wolves saw substance. That dingo *is everything*, not just because it moves through this world freely, but also because it stops to look only where it pleases.

I arrived at my old familiar stop and took the short walk to Sunbeam Estate, which had by then fallen into the hands of the conglomerate pillagers; it being a listed asset of Sunbeam Solutions, you see. I could hear the thumping music from out on the pavement, but only just. The front verandah was vibrating underfoot, but it wasn't until I opened the door that the full effect of ignorant complacence hit me head-on; that is to say, shit music, too loud. They had put in their soundproofing, all right, blocked out the windows as well, and there was a happening party underway. I realised that it was the last day of the co-working period and the keys were about to be handed over, if they hadn't been already, and apparently they had planned a festivity to mark the occasion.

The house was packed with fiendish-looking cunts doing drugs and shit, also necking one another for whatever reason, but the strangest sight that befell my eyes as I stood in the doorway and took it all in was Psycho-T, drinking water out of the fish tank through a bright pink silly straw, occasionally picking up his head to take fleeting breaths and scream praise to the heavens in the name of one *'Raël'*. Different strokes, I suppose.

I walked through to the kitchen and scanned the room. There were many familiar faces, but only one I cared about.

'What a sorry fucking sight,' I projected over the 'music'.

Sunbeam River, the man with the cheery smile and rosy outlook, was slumped over the bench with a fire engine in hand. *'A man with no suitcase big enough to carry his life.'*

He stood up straight.

'Surprised to see me?' I furthered.

'No,' he replied blandly. *'Come into my office.'*

We walked into the office that was no longer his; you could tell this by the lack of knickknacks on the desk. Quite a bare and boring sight, it was. I sat in the familiar place and Sunny stood, pretending to look out the window.

'I guess you came for your money.'

'You guess right,' I replied.

'You're not a bad kid, Eddy. Like I said when I hired you – smart, but not too smart. Who the fuck would have thought, you and Sandra. It would have work –'

'Whatever, dude, just open the fucking safe,' I interrupted, pointing to the framed *Warhol* (Campbell soup) print on the wall. I'd never actually seen behind that picture, but I'd always known that's where the safe was.

'I'm gonna miss this house,' he started. *'I'm gonna miss this business, too. You know –'*

'Shut your filthy mouth and open the damned safe, Sunny!' I half-yelled in my proudest voice.

He strolled across the room and punched in the combo. I considered rushing the cunt and taking all he had, but I wasn't sure I could make it back out the door in time; that big, skinny fuck was deceptively fast and strong, and I had learned what a skilled fighter he was when he insulted my shoes, so I decided on a more subtle approach.

'*I want more than five, gimme thirty.*'

'*I'll give you ten,*' he replied.

'*Twenty-five.*'

'*Ten.*'

'*Fifteen.*'

'*Twelve and a half.*'

'*Fuck you, deal,*' I replied.

He handed me my twelve-five and I walked out of the room without thanking him or looking back.

I considered leaving, having completed my primary objective, but I decided I was on a roll and went to Sandra's room instead.

In my flustering rush to leave two weeks prior, I had left my Chivas on the top shelf of her abhorrently littered closet, and I don't know why, but it had been weighing on my mind almost as much as the money. Maybe more.

I opened her door and walked in upon a mildly surprising scene. There she was, lying naked on the bed, far from lucidity. Her hair was messed up, her eyeliner running, her lipstick smudged (the first and only time I had seen her wear makeup), and she was covered in sweat and looking pale and sick, but probably most striking of all was that she happened to be getting fucked by six or seven different guys. Some of these humble gentlemen I knew – some were Sydney boys, some were regular customers, and there was also Alex from phone repair, and also the Marshmallow Man (she had always told me she found him utterly repulsive) – and some I didn't know.

This tangle of sensualist flesh and all the dicks in and around her was a sorry enough sight, but even worse were the ten or so guys leaning casually against the wall, watching and jerking and waiting for their turn. I went and grabbed my scotch – oddly disconnected from the situation – and tried to make a nonchalant exit, but when I heard …

'Eddy?'

... muttered from the mouth of the woman I had once loved, a mouth that had played host to Gan only knows how many swordfights that night, I turned around. She was disconnected, too.

'Eddy,' she repeated sweetly. *'You came back for me.'*

What a fucking farce that the most loving tone she had ever used with me was in the midst of all this. All motions stopped and all eyes fell upon us.

She tried to rise to a standing position, but her legs were jelly and the best she could do was to sit on the edge of the bed and look up at me.

'Kiss me,' she pleaded in a barely audible whisper.

I came to her, knelt down, and kissed her, reclaiming her heart, then I walked away, leaving her body to the wolves.

THE END.

Takani Dillon
15th January – 9th February 2020.
Brisbane.